U0025492

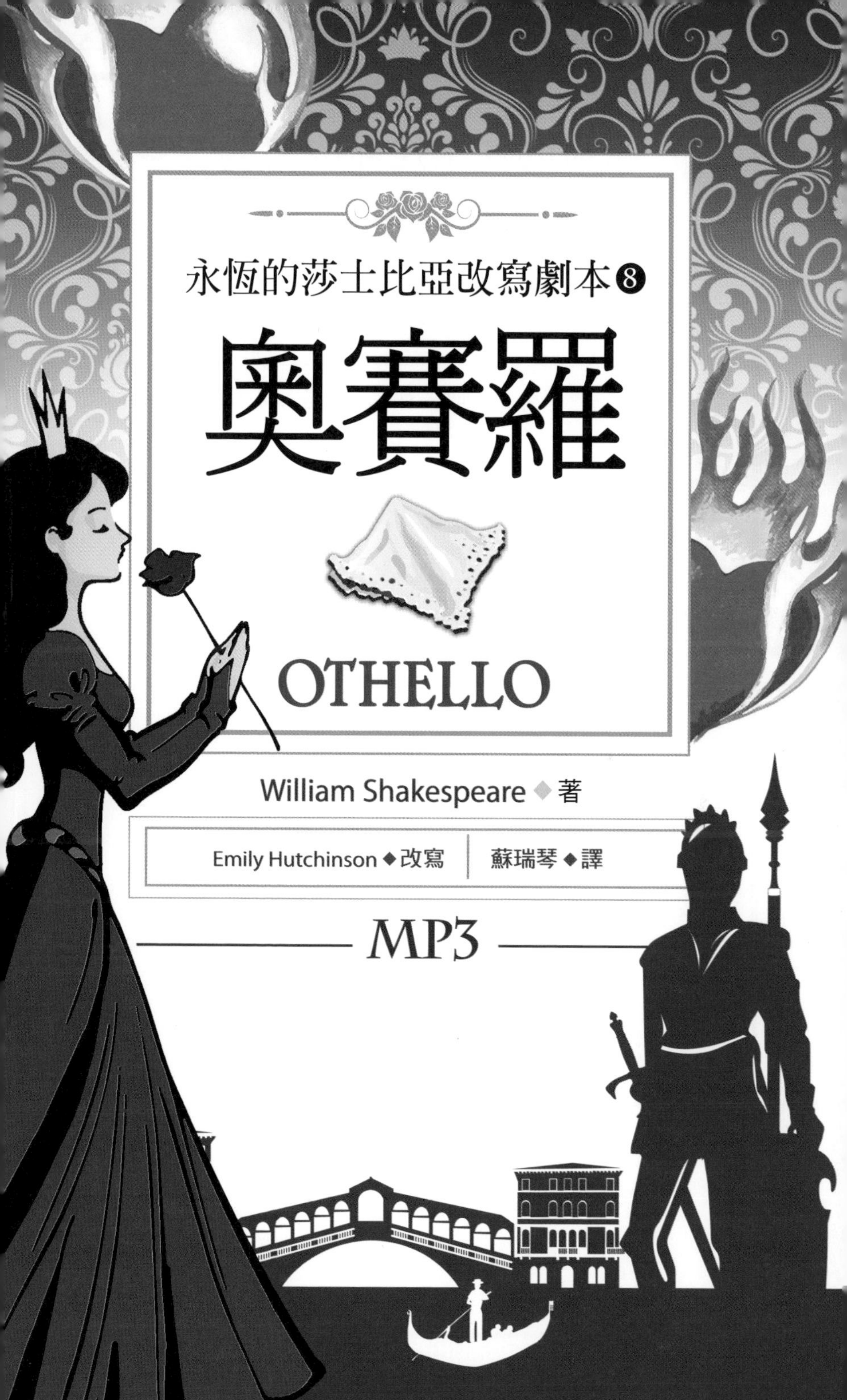

永恆的莎士比亞改寫劇本 8
奧賽羅
OTHELLO
William Shakespeare ◆ 著
Emily Hutchinson ◆ 改寫
蘇瑞琴 ◆ 譯
MP3

永恆的莎士比亞改寫劇本 ❽

奧賽羅

OTHELLO

作　　者	William Shakespeare, Emily Hutchinson
翻　　譯	蘇瑞琴
編　　輯	Gina Wang
校　　對	代雲芳
內文排版	劉秋筑
封面設計	林書玉
製程管理	洪巧玲
出 版 者	寂天文化事業股份有限公司
電　　話	+886-(0)2-2365-9739
傳　　真	+886-(0)2-2365-9835
網　　址	www.icosmos.com.tw
讀者服務	onlineservice@icosmos.com.tw
出版日期	2016 年 10 月 初版一刷

郵撥帳號 1998620-0 寂天文化事業股份有限公司
劃撥金額 600（含）元以上者，郵資免費。
訂購金額 600 元以下者，加收 65 元運費。
〔若有破損，請寄回更換，謝謝〕

國家圖書館出版品預行編目 (CIP) 資料

永恆的莎士比亞改寫劇本 .8 : 奧賽羅 / William Shakespeare, Emily Hutchinson 作 ; 蘇瑞琴譯 .
-- 初版 .-- [臺北市] : 寂天文化 , 2016.10
面 ;　公分
ISBN 978-986-318-508-6(平裝附光碟片)
873.43362　　105018059

Contents

Introduction

This play is set in Venice, Italy, and the island of Cyprus in the Mediterranean Sea. The time is the early 1600s. Othello, a Moor from northwest Africa, is the great army general of Venice. As the play opens, Othello's ensign Iago has been passed over for a promotion. Instead, Othello has promoted Cassio, a younger man. Iago is very angry. To get revenge, he plans to drive a wedge between Othello and his bride, Desdemona, by playing on Othello's jealousy. As the play continues, the noble Moor falls into Iago's trap, and tragedy follows.

Cast of Characters 2

DUKE OF VENICE

BRABANTIO: Desdemona's father, a senator

GRATIANO: Brabantio's brother; a noble Venetian

LODOVICO: a relative of Brabantio; a noble Venetian

OTHELLO: a noble Moor in the military service of Venice

CASSIO: Othello's honorable lieutenant

IAGO: Othello's ensign; a villain

RODERIGO: an easily fooled young gentleman

MONTANO: the governor of Cyprus before Othello

CLOWN: Othello's servant

DESDEMONA: Brabantio's daughter; Othello's fair young bride

EMILIA: Iago's wife

BIANCA: a prostitute

GENTLEMEN, SAILORS, OFFICERS, MESSENGER, HERALD, MUSICIANS, SERVANTS, and **SENATORS (SIGNIORS)**

ACT 1

Summary

奧賽羅提拔了凱西奧成為他的副將，此舉讓以阿哥很憤怒，他告訴羅德里戈他將為此事而報復奧賽羅。以阿哥想到一個方法，他要喚醒黛絲德夢娜的父親，告訴他奧賽羅已與他女兒私定終身。當氣急攻心的柏拉班修發現奧賽羅與黛絲德夢娜已成婚，他控訴奧賽羅用邪藥和巫術使女兒就範。

奧賽羅被迫為自己辯護，他描述自己與黛絲德夢娜間愛苗漸長的過程。黛絲德夢娜也在柏拉班修面前為奧賽羅的話作證，並表達她對丈夫的一片忠誠愛意。

奧賽羅必須前往賽浦勒斯島，抵禦土耳其人攻擊，黛絲德夢娜答應隨他而去。

以阿哥揭露他邪惡的計畫：他要藉由暗示奧賽羅，說黛絲德夢娜不忠，以引起奧賽羅的忌妒心。

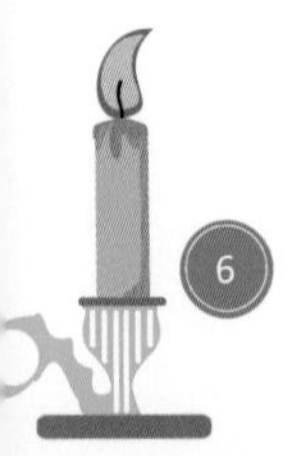

Scene 1

(Enter **Roderigo** and **Iago** on a street in Venice.)

RODERIGO: Why didn't you say so earlier?

IAGO: You never listen to me anyway.

RODERIGO: But you told me you hated him—

IAGO: I do. I deserve to be his lieutenant.
Yet he picked Michael Cassio instead.
Cassio has never proved himself in battle.
And I, who led men on many battlefields,
Will be Othello's mere ensign, the lowest rank of officer!

RODERIGO: I would rather be his hangman.

IAGO: A new system is in place.
It's who you know that counts—not what you can do.
Now, sir, judge for yourself whether I have any reason
To love the Moor.

RODERIGO: Why do you follow him, then?

IAGO: Don't be fooled. I only follow him to get back at him.

We can't all be in charge—nor can all those in charge be truly followed.
In following him, I'm looking out for my own good.
As heaven is my judge, I act not out of love and duty,
Even though I must make a show of service.
I am never what I seem to be.

RODERIGO: We can't let him get away with this!

IAGO: Let us wake up Desdemona's father.
Making him angry will lessen Othello's joy.

RODERIGO: Here is her father's house.

IAGO: Wake him! Yell as if the town is on fire!

RODERIGO: Hello! Brabantio! Signior Brabantio! Hello!

IAGO: Wake up, Brabantio! Thieves! Thieves!

BRABANTIO ***(appearing above, at a window)*****:** Why all the noise? What's wrong?

RODERIGO: Heavens, sir, you've been robbed!
Your heart is burst. You have lost half your soul.

Even now, an old black ram is mating with your white ewe.
Arise! Wake your neighbors with the bell,
Or else the devil may make you a grandfather.

BRABANTIO: Have you lost your mind? Who are you?

RODERIGO: I am Roderigo, sir. Don't you know my voice?

BRABANTIO: You are not welcome here!
I've told you my daughter is not for you.

RODERIGO: I have come to you with simple and pure reasons.

IAGO *(supporting Roderigo)*: We're here to help you. If you don't act quickly, your daughter will be mated with a Moorish horse. You'll have chargers for grandsons.

BRABANTIO: What kind of foul talk is that?

IAGO: It is the truth, sir. Your daughter and the Moor are now making the beast with two backs.

BRABANTIO: Villain! You'll answer for this.

RODERIGO: Sir, I will answer anything. Maybe it is your wish
That your fair daughter, in the middle of the night,
Has been carried off in the gross embrace of a lustful Moor.
If so, we must apologize for bothering you.
But if you did not know about it, then you should thank us.
Why don't you find out for yourself? If she is in her room or your house,
Bring the justice of the state against me for thus lying to you.

BRABANTIO: Give me a candle! Wake up the household!
Light, I say! Light!

(**He** exits from the balcony above.)

IAGO *(to Roderigo)***:** Farewell, for I must leave you.
It wouldn't help me to be used as a witness against Othello.

I know that he is in favor with the state.
Oh, he might get some slight punishment.
But the state needs him to lead in the Cyprus wars.
Though I hate him, I must show outward signs of love.
Bring the search party to the inn. I will be there with him. Farewell!

(**Iago** exits. **Brabantio** enters below. **Servants** carrying torches are with him.)

BRABANTIO: It is too true an evil. She is gone!
What's left of my life will be nothing but bitterness.
Now, Roderigo, where did you see her?
Oh, the foolish girl!
With the Moor, you said? Oh, treason of the blood!
How did you know it was she? Oh, she deceived me!
Wake up my family! Are they already married, do you think?

RODERIGO: Truly, I think they are.

BRABANTIO: Oh, heavens! How did she get out? Such deception!
Fathers, from now on, do not trust your daughters' minds
Based on how you see them act. Is there not magic
By which the nature of youth and virginity
May be abused? Haven't you, Roderigo, read of such things?

RODERIGO: Yes, sir, I have indeed.

BRABANTIO: Oh, if only she had been yours!
Do you know where we may find her and the Moor?

RODERIGO: I think I can find them.

BRABANTIO: Please, lead on! Good Roderigo, I'll reward you for this.

Scene 2

(**Othello**, **Iago**, and **servants** enter on another street.)

IAGO: Though I have killed men in war,
It goes against my conscience to commit murder.
I'm not evil enough to serve my own needs. Nine or ten times
I thought about stabbing Brabantio right here, under the ribs.

OTHELLO: It's better that you didn't.

IAGO: But he spoke rudely, insulting you.
I could hardly keep from attacking him!
But, I ask you, sir—are you married? You can be sure of this:
Brabantio will see that you are divorced,
Or bring whatever charges against you that the law allows.

OTHELLO: Let him do his worst.
The services that I have done for the state
Will speak louder than his complaints. No one knows this yet,

But when the right time comes, I will make it known that
I am descended from men of royal rank.
I can claim as great a fortune as my wife can.
Know this, Iago: If I didn't love the gentle Desdemona so much,
I would not have given up my freedom for all the treasure in the sea.
But look! What lights are coming this way?

(Enter **Cassio** and other **officers**, with **servants** carrying torches.)

IAGO: That's the awakened father and his friends! You'd better go in.

OTHELLO: No. I must be found. My talents, my title, and my perfect soul
Shall speak right of me. Is it they?

IAGO: I don't think so.

OTHELLO *(to Cassio's group)*: Greetings, friends! What is the news?

CASSIO: The duke sends greetings, General.
And wants to see you right away.

OTHELLO: What do you think is the matter?

CASSIO: Some news from Cyprus, I imagine.
Many important men are with the duke already.
They are calling for you, too.
When they did not find you at home,
The Senate sent three groups to find you.

OTHELLO: It's good that you have found me.
I must tell my household I am leaving.
Then I'll go with you. ***(He exits.)***

CASSIO *(to Iago)***:** Ensign, why is Othello here?

IAGO: To tell you the truth, he has boarded a rich vessel tonight.
If it turns out to be a lawful prize, he'll be rich for life.

CASSIO: I do not understand.

IAGO: He's married.

CASSIO: To whom?

(**Othello** re-enters.)

IAGO: Why, to—Come, captain, ready to go?

OTHELLO: I am ready.

CASSIO: Here's another troop looking for you.

(Enter **Brabantio**, **Roderigo**, and **officers** carrying torches and weapons.)

IAGO: It is Brabantio! General, be warned:
He comes with bad intentions.

OTHELLO: Hello! Stand right there!

RODERIGO ***(to Brabantio):*** Signior, it is the Moor.

BRABANTIO: Down with him, the thief!

(Both groups of men draw their swords.)

OTHELLO: Put away your bright swords.
The dew will rust them.
(to Brabantio): Good signior, it's better
to use the wisdom of your age
Than weapons to make your point.

BRABANTIO: Oh, you foul thief! Where have
you hidden my daughter?
You've put a spell on her. Why else would
a girl like her—
So tender, fair, and happy—be with you?
She has refused the best men in Venice.
Surely you have cast a foul spell on her!
You must have used drugs or minerals that
weaken the will.

Therefore, I arrest and charge you as a
Practicer of forbidden and illegal arts.

OTHELLO: Where must I go to answer this charge of yours?

BRABANTIO: To prison, until you are called to trial by the court.

OTHELLO: I will gladly obey. But what about the duke, who has sent these messengers ***(pointing to Cassio and his men)*** to bring me to him?

BRABANTIO: What? The duke is in council
At this time of the night? Let's go see him!
Mine is not a minor case.
The duke himself would feel this wrong
As if it were his own.
If, after such actions, you're allowed to go free,
Then bond-slaves and pagans shall our statesmen be.

Scene 3 5

(The **duke** and **senators** sit at a table in the council chamber.)

DUKE *(pointing to letters on the table)*: These reports tell different stories.

FIRST SENATOR: Indeed, they are quite different. Mine says 107 ships.

DUKE: My report says 140.

SECOND SENATOR: And mine says 200!
They don't agree about the number—
But they all agree that a Turkish fleet is approaching Cyprus.

DUKE: Yes, that news does seem clear.

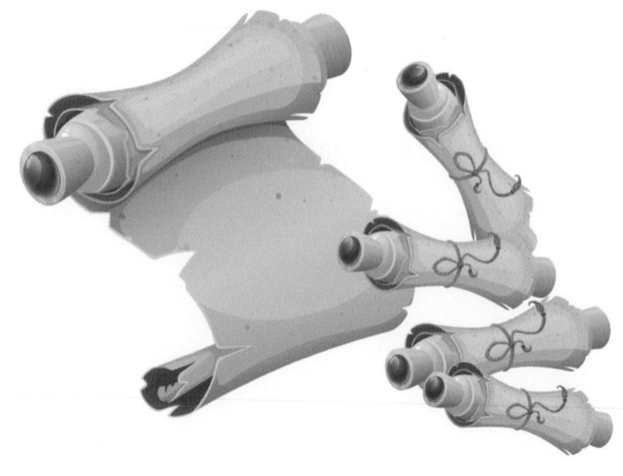

FIRST SENATOR: Here come Brabantio and the valiant Moor.

(Enter **Brabantio**, **Othello**, **Cassio**, **Iago**, **Roderigo**, and **officers**.)

DUKE: Valiant Othello, we must send you
Against our enemy, the Turks.
(to Brabantio): Oh! I did not see you.
Welcome, gentle signior. We missed
Your counsel and your help tonight.

BRABANTIO: And I missed yours.
Your good grace, pardon me.
Neither my position, nor anything I heard of your business
Has raised me from my bed.
Nor do public concerns take hold of me.
My particular grief is so intense it floods and swallows all other sorrows.

DUKE: Why? What's the matter?

BRABANTIO: My daughter! Oh, my daughter!

FIRST SENATOR: Dead?

BRABANTIO: Yes, to me!
She has been deceived, stolen from me, and corrupted

By spells and drugs bought from a quack.
It's against her nature to act like this—
So it must have been caused by witchcraft.

DUKE: I swear we shall punish whoever has done this—
Even if it is my own son.

BRABANTIO: I thank your grace humbly.
Here is the man—this Moor—the very man
Brought to you by your own messengers.

DUKE *(to Othello)*: What can you say to this?

OTHELLO: Most noble and honored signiors,
That I have taken this old man's daughter is true.
True, I have married her.
My offense is no greater than this.
I am not a gifted speaker. Yet, if I may,
I will tell the honest tale of my love and the mighty magic
(for this is what I am charged with)
I used to win his daughter.

BRABANTIO: This maiden was never bold.

Her spirit was so quiet that she blushed at everything.
I therefore say again that he used some powerful drug on her.

DUKE: To swear this does not prove it.
Without some proof, you can hardly speak against him.

OTHELLO: I ask you to send for the lady.
Let her speak of me before her father.
If her report of me is evil, take away the honors you've given me.
Then, let your sentence fall upon my life.

DUKE: Bring Desdemona here.

(Two or three men exit.)

OTHELLO ***(to Iago)*****:** Ensign, lead them. You know where she is.

(**Iago** exits.)

(to the duke and senators)**:** Until she gets here, I shall tell you
How this fair lady and I fell in love.
Her father loved me and often invited me to his home.

He asked me for the story of my life.
I told of my dangerous travels, of terrible
accidents in floods and on the field.
I told of being taken prisoner by enemies
And sold into slavery.
I spoke of my escape and my adventures
in vast caves and idle deserts.
Desdemona listened carefully until
household duties would call her away.
Whenever she could, she'd come again,
And with a greedy ear devour my story.
One day, I found a convenient time
And told her my story all at once.
Before this, she had only heard it in bits.
She often cried when I spoke of my youth.
My strange and sad story done, she said
she wished that heaven had made such a
man for her.
She said, if I had a friend who loved her,
I should teach him how to tell my story.
That alone would woo her.
I took her hint and spoke up for myself.
She loved me because of the dangers I had
experienced.

I loved her because she was so moved by them.
This is the only witchcraft I have used.
Here comes the lady. Let her speak for herself.

(Enter **Desdemona**, **Iago**, and **attendants**.)

DUKE *(aside)*: I think this tale would win my daughter, too!
Good Brabantio, you'll have to make the best of it.

BRABANTIO: I beg you, hear her speak.
If she says that she was half the wooer,
May I be punished for my unjust blame of Othello!
(to Desdemona): Come here, gentle lady.
Do you see the person to whom
You owe the most obedience?

DESDEMONA: I see here a divided duty, my noble father.
I owe you for my life and education,
For I am your daughter.
But here stands my husband.
As much duty as my mother showed

To you, preferring you before her father,
So I must now show to the Moor, my lord.

BRABANTIO *(to Desdemona)*: God be with you!
I'm done with it.

DUKE *(to Brabantio)*: Let me say something
To help you accept these lovers.
To grieve over a misfortune that is past
Is the surest way to more misfortunes.
A robbed person who smiles
steals something from the thief;
He robs himself who cries a pointless
grief.
Now we must proceed to affairs of state.
The Turks are heading for Cyprus.
Othello, you are the best man to go there
and defend it for us.

OTHELLO: I will. But my wife will need a
proper home.

DUKE: If it please you, let it be at her father's.

BRABANTIO: I will not have it so!

OTHELLO: Nor I.

DESDEMONA: Nor I. Let me go with Othello.

OTHELLO: Let her have your permission.
If I neglect my duties when she is with me,
Let housewives make a skillet of my helmet
And evil attack my good name!

DUKE: It's up to you if she stays or goes.
The business in Cyprus is urgent.
Othello, you must leave in one hour.
(to Brabantio): And, noble signior, if virtue is a sign of beauty,
Your son-in-law is far more fair than black!

BRABANTIO *(to Othello)***:** Watch her, Moor.
She has deceived her father, and may deceive you, too.

(**Brabantio**, **duke**, **senators**, and **officers** exit.)

OTHELLO: I'd stake my life on her fidelity!
Honest Iago, I must leave my Desdemona to your care
Until she is ready to follow me.

Let your wife attend to her, and bring them both along when the time is best.
Come, Desdemona. We have but an hour,
And must obey the time.

(**Othello** and **Desdemona** exit.)

RODERIGO: Iago, what should I do?

IAGO: Why, go to bed and sleep.

RODERIGO: I will go and drown myself.

IAGO: How silly you are!

RODERIGO: It is foolish to live when living is torment.

IAGO: Come, be a man! Drown yourself? Drown cats and blind puppies! I am speaking as your friend. Put money in your purse. Go to the wars. Before long, Desdemona will grow tired of the Moor. Othello is too old for her. She will look for someone younger. Therefore, make all the money you can. She will soon be yours Forget about drowning yourself. Take your chances on being hanged for trying to get what you want. A pox on drowning!

RODERIGO: Are you sure of this?

IAGO: You can count on it. Go, make money! I have told you often, and I tell you again—I hate the Moor. I hate him from the bottom of my heart. You have no less reason to hate him. Let us help each other get revenge against him. We'll talk more about this tomorrow at my lodging.

RODERIGO: I'll be there early.

IAGO: Go on, good night. No more talk of drowning, do you hear?

RODERIGO: I am changed. I'll sell all my land.

(**Roderigo** exits.)

IAGO: This is how I profit off a fool!
I have good reason to hate the Moor.
Gossip says that he seduced my wife.
The hint is enough to make me believe it.
Othello thinks well of me.
That will make my revenge easier.
Cassio's a handsome man with fine manners. Let me see now—how can I use that to my advantage?

Yes, I'll suggest to Othello
That Cassio is too familiar with his wife.
Men who look like Cassio are built to
  make women turn unfaithful.
The Moor is of a free and open nature.
He thinks a man is good if he seems so.
Yes, he will be easily fooled.
I have it! It is decided! Hell and night
Must bring this wicked plan to light.

(Exit.)

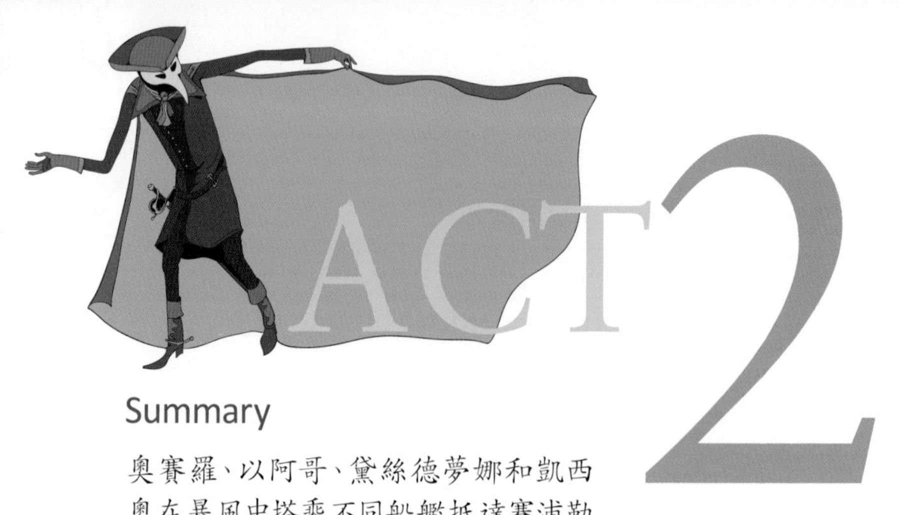

Summary

奧賽羅、以阿哥、黛絲德夢娜和凱西奧在暴風中搭乘不同船艦抵達賽浦勒斯。暴風摧毀土耳其軍隊的船隻，因此奧賽羅與土耳其一戰已然告終。以阿哥開始進行邪惡的計畫，他暗示羅德里戈，說黛絲德夢娜與凱西奧相戀。由於羅德里戈也愛上黛絲德夢娜，他答應激怒凱西奧，並使他名譽掃地。

當晚，以阿哥將凱西奧灌醉，而羅德里戈激怒酒醉的凱西奧讓他出手打人。當奧賽羅得知此事之後，以阿哥聲稱那是凱西奧的錯，凱西奧被解除副將一職。凱西奧因名聲掃地而感到苦惱，他去找以阿哥聊天。以阿哥建議他請黛絲德夢娜幫助他，而凱西奧也同意這麼做。以阿哥內心竊喜，因為他打算讓奧賽羅誤會凱西奧與黛絲德夢娜相戀。

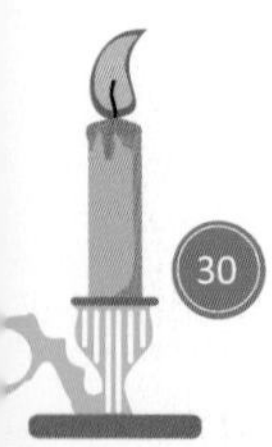

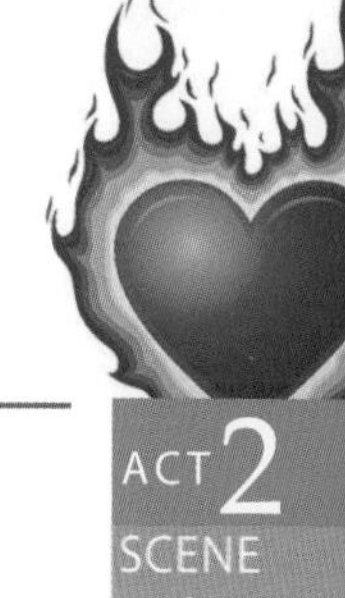

Scene 1 6

(**Montano** and **two gentlemen** enter a seaport in Cyprus as a storm rages.)

MONTANO: I have never seen a worse storm.
What do you think will happen?

SECOND GENTLEMAN: The Turkish fleet is sure to be destroyed.
It will be impossible to survive this.

(Enter a **third gentleman**.)

THIRD GENTLEMAN: News, lads! Our wars are done!
These angry waters have destroyed the Turks' ships.
A noble ship of Venice has sighted the terrible wrecks and the sufferings
Of most of the Turkish fleet. That ship has landed here, and
A man from Verona has come on shore.
He is Michael Cassio, lieutenant to the warlike Moor.
The Moor himself is still at sea and on his way here.

MONTANO: I'm glad to hear it. Othello will be a worthy governor.

THIRD GENTLEMAN: But Cassio, though he tells good news about the Turkish loss,
Is very worried about the Moor.

MONTANO: Let us pray that he is safe.

(Enter **Cassio**.)

CASSIO: Thank you, valiant men of this war-torn island
Who so honor the Moor! Oh, let the heavens keep him safe!

MONTANO: Is his ship a good one?

CASSIO: His ship is strong, and his pilot has expert skills.

(Offstage, a voice cries, "A sail, a sail, a sail!")

CASSIO ***(to second gentleman)*****:** Sir, go see who is arriving.

SECOND GENTLEMAN: I shall. ***(He exits.)***

MONTANO: Good lieutenant, is your general married?

CASSIO: Yes. To a woman whose beauty and reputation are flawless.

(Re-enter **second gentleman**.)

SECOND GENTLEMAN: Iago, ensign to the general, has landed.

CASSIO: That's good. He has with him the divine Desdemona.

MONTANO: Who is she?

CASSIO: Othello's good wife.

She was left in Iago's protection.

Now may the heavens bring Othello safely to Desdemona's arms.

(Enter **Desdemona**, **Emilia**, **Iago**, **Roderigo**, and **attendants**.)

Greetings to you, lady! May the grace of heaven surround you.

DESDEMONA: Thank you, Cassio. What news do you have of my husband?

CASSIO: I know only that he is well and will soon be here.

DESDEMONA: Oh, but I'm afraid! How did your ships get separated?

CASSIO: The storm parted us. But listen!

(Offstage a voice cries, "A sail, a sail!")

CASSIO: Go see who's coming.

(**Second gentleman** exits.)

(to Iago): Good ensign, you are welcome.

(to Emilia): Welcome, madam.

(Cassio kisses the hand of Emilia. Then he kisses the hand of Desdemona.)

(to Iago): I hope this doesn't bother you, good Iago. It's my upbringing That teaches me to make such a bold show of courtesy.

IAGO *(to himself)*: Good! He kisses her hand. In such a little web, I can catch a fly as big as Cassio. Yes, smile at her—go ahead! I'll catch you in your own courtesy. If your actions make you lose your position, you'll wish you hadn't been such a courtly gentleman! Very good. Well kissed! What lovely manners!

(A trumpet blows offstage.)

(to Cassio): It's the Moor! I know his trumpet.

(Enter **Othello** and **attendants**.)

OTHELLO: Oh, my soul's joy!

DESDEMONA: My dear Othello!

(Othello kisses Desdemona.)

IAGO ***(aside)*****:** Oh, you are in tune with each other now!
But I'll untune the strings that make this music, as honest as I am.

OTHELLO: Come, let's go to the castle.
News, friends! Our wars are done. The Turks are drowned.
(to Desdemona): You'll be well-loved in Cyprus, my dear—
I've found great affection here.

(**Everyone** but **Iago** and **Roderigo** exits.)

IAGO ***(to Roderigo)*****:** Meet me soon at the harbor. Be sure to come. Cassio keeps watch on the guardhouse tonight. But first, I must tell you this: Desdemona is madly in love with him.

RODERIGO: With Cassio? Why, it isn't possible!

IAGO: Keep quiet, and just listen to me. Remember how violently she first loved the Moor? And just because he bragged and told her fantastic lies? Will she keep loving him just to hear his babbling? Don't you believe it. She needs a man who is closer to her own age. Nature itself will force her to seek someone new. Cassio is the obvious choice. He's a very flattering rascal. Besides, he's handsome! He has all those qualities that foolish and young minds look for. He's a completely rotten rascal. And the woman has fallen for him already!

RODERIGO: I cannot believe that about her. She has a blessed character.

IAGO: Blessed, my eye! If she was truly blessed, she would never have loved the Moor. Blessed, my foot! Didn't you see Cassio kissing her hand?

RODERIGO: Yes, I did. It was just courtesy.

IAGO: It was lechery, I tell you! Their lips were so close their very breaths embraced! Bah! But, sir, do as I say. Watch carefully tonight. Cassio does not know you. Find some way to make him angry. Talk too loud, or say something to offend him—whatever you can think of at the time. He is very short-tempered. Maybe he'll try to hit you. Provoke him to that, if you can. That's all I need to start a mutiny against Cassio and have him thrown out of Cyprus. That way, you'll have a quicker route to Desdemona. But first, we must remove the one obstacle that stands in front of both of us.

RODERIGO: I will do this, if it will give me any advantage.

IAGO: I guarantee it! Meet me soon at the castle. Goodbye.

RODERIGO: Goodbye. ***(Exit Roderigo.)***

IAGO *(aside)*: I really do believe that Cassio loves her. It is natural and likely that she loves him, too.

As much as I hate him, the Moor
Has a faithful, loving, and noble nature.
I'm sure he'll be a dear husband to her.
Now, I love her, too—but not completely out of lust.
I love her because she'll help me get revenge,
Since I suspect the lusty Moor has seduced my wife.
The thought of that gnaws at my insides.
Nothing will satisfy me until Othello and I are even, wife for wife.
If I fall short of that, I'll still make him
So jealous that good sense won't cure him.
To get this done, the worthless Venetian, Roderigo,

Must do what I've told him. Then I'll
  have Michael Cassio in my pocket
(for I'm afraid that Cassio, too, has been
  in my marriage bed)
And the Moor will thank me, love me,
  and reward me
For making a complete fool of him!
That's the plan, though it's still a bit confused.
Evil's face is not clear until it's too late.

Scene 2 7

(A **herald**, with a proclamation, enters a street.)

HERALD: It is Othello's wish that everyone celebrate the drowning of the Turkish fleet. Some should dance, and some make bonfires. But everyone should have fun because this is also his wedding celebration! All kitchens are open. There is free feasting from the present hour of five until the bell rings eleven. Heaven bless the island of Cyprus and our noble General Othello!

(**All** exit.)

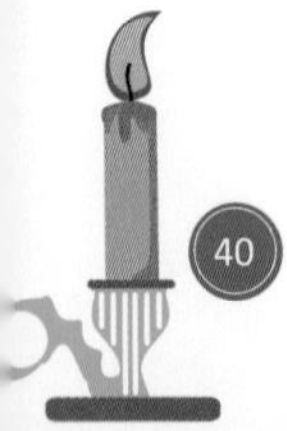

Scene 3

(At the castle. Enter **Othello**, **Desdemona**, **Cassio**, and **attendants**.)

OTHELLO: Good Cassio, you are in charge of the guard tonight.
Make sure that the celebrations do not get out of hand. Goodnight for now.
(to Desdemona): Come, my dear love.

(Exit **Othello**, **Desdemona**, and **attendants**. Enter **Iago**.)

CASSIO: Welcome, Iago. We must go on watch now.

IAGO: Not so soon, lieutenant. It's not ten yet! I have some wine. Let us drink to the health of black Othello.

CASSIO: I have already had too much wine. I can't overdo it with any more.

IAGO: What? This is a night of rejoicing. Some friends are waiting to join us. Go, call them in.

CASSIO: I'll do it—but I don't like the idea.

(Exit **Cassio**.)

IAGO *(aside)*: He must drink one more cup
On top of what he's already had tonight.
That will make him quicker to argue and take offense.
That lovesick fool Roderigo has already been toasting Desdemona tonight.
He's drained many cups to the bottom
When he's supposed to be on guard.
Three boys of Cyprus, whom I've made drunk with flowing wine,
Are on guard, too. Now, among all these drunkards
I'll provoke Cassio to some action
That will cause offense on the island. But here they come!

(Enter **Cassio**, **Montano**, and **gentlemen**. **Servants** follow with wine.)

CASSIO: By God, I've had a huge cup already.

MONTANO: Come now! It's just a little one, no more than a pint.

IAGO: Some wine over here!

(Iago sings a few drinking songs, which Cassio admires. The men continue drinking and toasting Othello's health.

At last, Cassio gets ready to leave.)

CASSIO: Let us see to our business. Do not think, gentlemen, that I am drunk. ***(pointing to Iago)***: This is my ensign. ***(holding up each hand)***: This is my right hand, and this is my left. I am not drunk now. I can stand and speak well enough.

(**Cassio** exits, obviously drunk.)

MONTANO: Come, gentlemen, it's time to begin the watch.

IAGO ***(pointing in Cassio's direction)*****:** You see him?
Cassio is a soldier fit to stand beside Caesar and give orders.
But take a look at this vice of his.
It is the exact equal of his virtue—one is as strong as the other.
Because of Cassio's weakness, I fear that the trust Othello puts in him
Will one day cause trouble on this island.

MONTANO: But is he like this very often?

IAGO: Always, before he goes to bed.
He'd be awake all night if his drinking didn't put him to sleep.

MONTANO: Does the general know? It would be a good idea to tell him about this.

(Enter **Roderigo**.)

IAGO *(aside to Roderigo)*: What are you doing here, Roderigo?
Go after the lieutenant!

(Exit **Roderigo**.)

MONTANO: It's a pity that the noble Moor
Should have a weak man in such an important position.
It would be wise to say so to the Moor.

IAGO: I wouldn't do it for this entire fair island!
I love Cassio very much. I will try to help him with his problem.
But listen! What's that noise?

(A voice from offstage cries "Help!" Enter **Cassio**, chasing **Roderigo**.)

CASSIO: Damn, you villain! You rascal!

MONTANO: What's the matter, Lieutenant?

CASSIO: Do I need a villain to teach me my duty?
I'll beat this knave to teach him his place!

RODERIGO: Beat me?

CASSIO: Still chattering? ***(He strikes Roderigo.)***

MONTANO: No, Cassio! ***(He grabs Cassio by the arm.)*** Stop fighting.

CASSIO: Let go of me, sir, or I'll knock you over the head.

MONTANO: Come, come, you're drunk!

CASSIO: Drunk? ***(Montano and Cassio fight.)***

IAGO ***(aside to Roderigo)*****:** Away, I say! Go warn everyone of a mutiny.

(**Roderigo** exits.)

Stop fighting, good lieutenant. For God's sake, gentlemen!

(Offstage, a bell rings to wake the town. **Othello** and **attendants** enter.)

OTHELLO: What's the matter here? How did this brawl get started?
Have we turned into Turks? Are we doing to ourselves
What heaven stopped the Turks from doing? Speak up. Who started this?

IAGO: I do not know. They were friends just a moment ago.
Then, the next moment, their swords were out and pointed at each other
In a bloody fight. I can't tell you how it started.

OTHELLO: Cassio, how did you get involved?

CASSIO: Please, pardon me. I cannot speak.

OTHELLO: Montano, what happened?

MONTANO: Worthy Othello, I am hurt badly. I was only defending myself.

OTHELLO: Now, I want to know how this fight started and who caused it.
The one who is proved at fault—even if

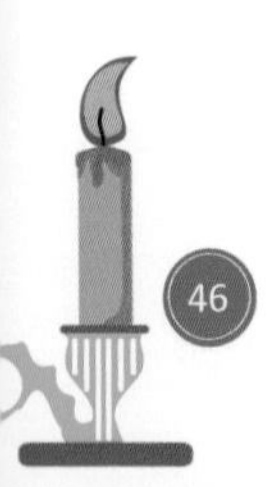

he were my twin brother—
Will lose my friendship. This is outrageous! Iago, who started it?

IAGO: I'd rather have my tongue cut out
Than to say anything against Michael Cassio.
Still, I believe that speaking the truth shall not harm him.
So here it is, General. Montano and I were talking here.
Then a fellow came crying out for help.
Cassio was following him with a drawn sword, trying to kill him.
Sir, as Montano and I tried to stop Cassio,
the other fellow ran away.
I tried to catch up to him, but he outran me. I came back here quickly,
Because I heard the clanking of swords and Cassio swearing loudly.
Until tonight, I could never have said this about him.
But men are only men—even the best men sometimes slip.

I believe that Cassio must have received some sort of insult
From the man who ran away. It was beyond his patience to let it go.

OTHELLO: Iago, it is your honesty and love that lead you to excuse Cassio.
Cassio, I love you—but you will serve as my officer no longer.

(Enter **Desdemona**, with **attendants**.)

DESDEMONA: What's the matter, dear?

OTHELLO: All's well now, sweetheart. Come away to bed.
(to Montano): Sir, my doctor will take care of your injuries.
(to attendants): Lead him away.

(**Montano** exits, with **attendants**.)

Iago, calm down any who have been
distracted by this brawl.
Come, Desdemona,
It's the story of a soldier's life
To have peaceful sleep disturbed by strife.

(**All** but **Iago** and **Cassio** exit.)

IAGO: Have you been hurt, Lieutenant?

CASSIO: Yes, beyond all hope of a cure.

IAGO: Oh, God forbid!

CASSIO: Reputation, reputation, reputation!
Oh, I have lost my reputation!

IAGO: Reputation is a foolish thing, often got without merit and lost without deserving. Come on, man! You can quickly recover the general's good graces. Appeal to him—he'll listen.

CASSIO: I'd rather ask him to hate me than forgive such a weak and drunken officer. Drunk? Babble? Fighting? Swearing? Oh, you invisible spirit of wine, let us call you the devil!

IAGO: Who was the man you were fighting? What had he done to you?

CASSIO: I don't know. I remember nothing clearly.

IAGO: Why, you seem well enough now. How did you recover so fast?

CASSIO: The devil of drunkenness has given way to the devil of anger. One flaw leads me to another. Oh, I hate myself!

IAGO: Don't be so hard on yourself. I wish all of this hadn't happened. But since it has, make the best of it.

CASSIO: If I ask him for my position again, he'll accuse me as a drunkard!

IAGO: I'll tell you what you should do. The general's wife has a great deal of influence over him. Ask for her help. She is so free, so kind, so good. She thinks it is wrong not to do more than people ask her to do. I'll bet my fortune that she will help you!

CASSIO: You give me good advice.

IAGO: I promise you, it comes to you out of sincere love and honest kindness.

CASSIO: I believe you. In the morning, I will beg for Desdemona's help.

IAGO: You're doing the right thing. Good night, now.

CASSIO: Good night, honest Iago.

(**Cassio** exits.)

IAGO *(aside)*: How would anyone say I'm a villain when I give such good advice?
Winning Desdemona's support
Is Cassio's only hope. But while she is pleading with the Moor,

I'll pour poison into his ear. I'll say she
Speaks only out of lust for Cassio.
The more good she tries to do for him,
The worse she'll look in the eyes of the Moor.
In this way, I will turn her virtue into
  wickedness.
Out of her goodness, I'll make the net to
catch them all!

(Enter **Roderigo**.)

What is it, Roderigo?

RODERIGO: I've been thoroughly beaten tonight. I have nothing but experience to show for all my pains. My money is almost spent. So I'll soon have to return to Venice.

IAGO: How pathetic are those who have no
  patience!
What wound ever healed but by degrees?
Cassio may have beaten you, but you have
  ruined Cassio.
Be patient. Go to bed now. You'll know
  more soon. Go on!

(**Roderigo** exits.)

Two things must be done. My wife must speak to Desdemona about Cassio while I work on the Moor.
I'll bring Othello in just when Cassio is appealing to Desdemona.
Yes, that's the way!
I won't spoil this plan by any delay.

(**Iago** exits.)

Summary

黛絲德夢娜答應幫助凱西奧，當她開始替凱西奧求情，希望奧賽羅能恢復凱西奧的職位，以阿哥卻一直暗示奧賽羅，說黛絲德夢娜和凱西奧有婚外情。

艾米莉亞撿到黛絲德夢娜的手帕，她雖不知道為何以阿哥要求她偷這條手帕，她還是將手帕交給以阿哥。以阿哥將手帕放在凱西奧房內。當奧賽羅告訴以阿哥她需要黛絲德夢娜不忠的證據，以阿哥說他看見凱西奧用黛絲德夢娜的手帕擦鬍子。

稍後，當奧賽羅向黛絲德夢娜問起手帕，她改變了話題，想跟奧賽羅談凱西奧和他的職位。奧賽羅此時已深信黛絲德夢娜出軌，憤而離去。凱西奧去找畢昂嘉，請她仿作他在房裡找到的手帕刺繡圖樣。

Scene 1 9

(Enter **Cassio** and **Iago** in front of the castle on Cyprus.)

CASSIO: Iago, will you ask your wife to arrange a meeting with Desdemona?

IAGO: I'll send for Emilia now. Then I'll distract the Moor.

CASSIO: I humbly thank you. ***(Exit Iago.)***
You are a kind and honest man.

(Enter **Emilia**.)

EMILIA: Good day, good lieutenant. I am sorry about what happened to you.
But all will be well soon. Desdemona has been speaking in your favor.

CASSIO: Still, I beg you to give me a chance to speak to her alone.

EMILIA: Please come in, then, sir. I will take you to her.

CASSIO: I am indebted to you for this.

(**Emilia** and **Cassio** exit.)

Scene 2

(Enter **Desdemona**, **Cassio**, and **Emilia** in the garden of the castle.)

DESDEMONA: Be assured, good Cassio, that I will do what I can for you.

CASSIO: Dear lady, I shall always be your faithful servant.

DESDEMONA: I know that, and I thank you. You can count on me.

If I promise something out of friendship, I do it to the last detail.

My lord won't get any rest. I'll wear down his patience.

In everything he does, I'll mix in talk about your position.

So cheer up, Cassio. I would rather die than let you down.

(Enter **Othello** and **Iago**.)

CASSIO: Madam, I'll leave now.

DESDEMONA: Why, stay and hear what I say.

CASSIO: Not now, madam. I am very uncomfortable with this.

DESDEMONA: Well, do what you think best.

(Exit **Cassio**.)

IAGO: Ha! I don't like that.

OTHELLO: What did you say?

IAGO: Nothing, my lord.

OTHELLO: Wasn't that Cassio with my wife?

IAGO: Cassio, my lord? No, surely he would not sneak away
So guilty-like when he saw you coming.

OTHELLO: I do believe it was he.

DESDEMONA: Greetings, my lord! I have been talking to Cassio.
If I have any power to influence you, accept his apology at once.
He truly loves you! If not, I can't judge an honest face.
Please, give him back his position.

OTHELLO: Not now, sweet Desdemona. We'll speak of this another time.

DESDEMONA: Please, dear, name the time! Let it not be more than three days.

He's truly sorry for his mistake. You know, if you asked anything of me,
I would do it for you. Why do you deny my simple request?

OTHELLO: Please, say no more.
He can come to me when he wants to.
I will deny you nothing!
Now, I ask you to do this:
Please leave me alone for a little while.

DESDEMONA: Shall I deny you? No! Farewell, my lord.

(Exit **Desdemona** and **Emilia**.)

OTHELLO: Excellent wretch! The devil take my soul, but I really do love you!

IAGO: My noble lord—

OTHELLO: What is it, Iago?

IAGO: When you wooed my lady, did Cassio know of your love for her?

OTHELLO: He did, from beginning to end. Why do you ask?

IAGO: Oh, I was just wondering.

OTHELLO: Wondering about what, Iago?

IAGO: I did not think he had known her.

OTHELLO: Oh, yes. He often carried messages between us.

IAGO: Indeed?

OTHELLO: Yes, indeed! Do you see something wrong with that?
Please, tell me what's on your mind. Give me your worst thoughts.

IAGO: You ask me to tell my thoughts, good lord?
What if they are rotten and false? Who has such a pure heart
That unclean ideas do not sometimes creep in?

OTHELLO: You are hurting your friend, Iago, if you think he's been wronged
And fail to tell him what you think.

IAGO: Since I may be mistaken, I'd rather
keep my thoughts to myself.

OTHELLO: What do you mean?

IAGO: A man or a woman's good name,
my dear lord,
Is the most important jewel of the soul.
Who steals my purse steals trash. It was
something, now it's nothing.
It was mine, now it's his. It has belonged
to thousands of others.
But he who takes from me my good name
Robs me of that which does not enrich
him, and makes me poor indeed.

OTHELLO: By heaven, I demand to know what
you are thinking!

IAGO: Beware, my lord, of jealousy!
It is a green-eyed monster that laughs at
the meat it eats.
It is better for a man to know for sure that
his wife has been unfaithful
Than to merely suspect it. How time
drags on for the man

Who adores, but doubts; suspects, yet loves deeply!

OTHELLO: Why do you say this? You can't make me jealous
By saying my wife is lovely, eats well, loves company,
Speaks freely, sings, and dances well. In a virtuous person, these are but more virtues.
Though I am not perfect, I will not doubt her love. She had eyes, and she chose me. No, Iago,
I must see evidence before I doubt. And when I doubt, I must have proof.
When there's proof, that's the end of it.
No more love or jealousy!

IAGO: I'm glad to hear this. I have no proof, but
Watch your wife! Observe her well when she is with Cassio.
Remember that she deceived her father by marrying you.
He thought it was witchcraft—but I should say no more.

I beg your pardon for being too concerned about you.

OTHELLO: I am grateful for your concern.

IAGO: I hope you realize that I spoke only out of love.
But I see that you're disturbed.
I beg you not to jump to conclusions.
Suspecting something does not make it true.

OTHELLO: I do not think that Desdemona is anything but honest.

IAGO: And long may she live so! And long may you live to think so!

OTHELLO: And yet—

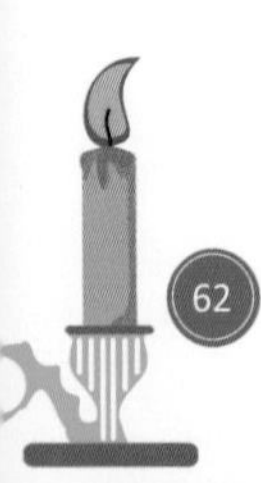

IAGO: Yes, there's one other point.
All things in nature tend to mate
With those who are like themselves.
But she did not.
One might smell in that kind of desire unnatural thoughts.
But forgive me—I'm not exactly talking about her.
Although I do fear that her better judgment might cause her to
Compare you with men of her own race and later reject you.

OTHELLO: Farewell, farewell! If you see anything else, let me know.
Tell your wife to observe, too. Now, I want to be alone, Iago.

IAGO: My lord, I'll take my leave. ***(Iago starts to walk away.)***

OTHELLO ***(to himself)*****:** Why did I marry?
Iago, this honest man, no doubt sees and
Knows more—much more—than he says.

IAGO ***(returning)*****:** My lord, give this time.
Nothing is proven yet.

But keep an eye on Cassio.
Watch if your lady pleads in his favor
Too strongly or too often.
Much will be seen in that.
Meanwhile, just think of my fears as foolish and consider her innocent.

OTHELLO: Don't worry about me.

IAGO: Once again, I take my leave.

(Exit **Iago**.)

OTHELLO: This fellow is exceedingly honest.
He knows all types of people.
If he is right about Desdemona, I'll send her packing.
Perhaps, because I am black, or because I am older than she is,
She has betrayed me.
Oh, what a curse marriage is,
That we can call these delicate creatures ours and not control them!
I'd rather be a toad living in a dungeon
Than have a part of something I love used by others. Oh! Here comes Desdemona.

(Re-enter **Desdemona** and **Emilia**.)

If she is false, then heaven mocks itself! I won't believe it.

DESDEMONA: How are you, my dear Othello?

OTHELLO: I have a pain in my forehead, here.

DESDEMONA: Why, that must be because you haven't had enough sleep.

Let me tie my handkerchief around your head. That will help.

OTHELLO: Your handkerchief is too little. ***(He pushes it away, and it drops to the floor.)***

Let it alone. Come, I'll go in with you.

DESDEMONA: I am sorry that you are not well.

(Exit **Othello** and **Desdemona**.)

EMILIA ***(picking up the handkerchief)*****:** I am glad to have found this.

This was her first gift from the Moor.

Iago has asked me 100 times to steal it.

But she loves it so much she always carries it,

Since Othello made her promise to always keep it.

What Iago wants with it, heaven knows;
I don't.
I want only to please him. ***(Re-enter Iago.)***

IAGO: Hello! What are you doing here alone?

EMILIA: I have something for you—that handkerchief you wanted.

IAGO: Have you stolen it from her?

EMILIA: Of course not. It was dropped by accident, and I picked it up.

IAGO: Good woman! Give it to me.

EMILIA: What will you do with it?

IAGO ***(grabbing it)*****:** Why, what is it to you?

EMILIA: If it's not for something important, give it back to me.
The poor lady will go crazy when she realizes she's lost it.

IAGO: Don't let on that you know anything.
I have use for it. Go, leave me.

(Exit **Emilia**.)

I'll put this handkerchief in Cassio's room and let him find it.
Little things like this are quite convincing to the jealous mind.
The Moor is already influenced by my poisonous words.
Dangerous ideas are poisonous in their nature.
At first they do not taste too bad, but soon they get into the blood
And burn like sulfur.

(Re-enter **Othello**.)

Greetings, my lord!

OTHELLO: Unfaithful! What did I know of her stolen hours of lust?
I didn't see it, didn't think of it, and wasn't harmed by it.
I slept well, ate well, and was free and merry.
I didn't know that the villain Cassio had been kissing her.
I'd have been happy if the whole army had made love to her—as long as I didn't know.
Now I must say farewell to peace of mind! Farewell to happiness!

IAGO: Is it possible, my lord?

OTHELLO: You'd better be sure of it, Iago.
Give me visible proof!
Or, by my eternal soul, you'd be better off to be born a dog
Than to answer my awakened wrath!

IAGO: Oh, God! Oh, heaven forgive me! Oh, monstrous world!
Take note, take note, world: To be direct and honest is not safe.

I thank you for teaching me this lesson. From now on,
I'll love no friend, since love causes such offense.

OTHELLO: No, stay. You should be honest.
By all the world, I believe my wife to be honest, and believe she is not.
I think that you are truthful, and think that you are not.
I must have some proof. Her name, which was as clean
As Diana's face, is now grimy and black as my own face.
I wish I could be certain!

IAGO: I see, sir, you are eaten up with passion.
I am sorry that I caused this.
Do you want to be sure?

OTHELLO: Want to be? No, I will be!

IAGO: But how?
How will you be certain, my lord?
Do you want to see her in the act?

OTHELLO: Death and damnation! Oh!

IAGO: It would be very difficult to catch them. How then?

OTHELLO: Give me absolute proof she's been unfaithful. I'll tear her to pieces!

IAGO: I do not like being in this position.
But I'll tell you this:
I heard Cassio talking in his sleep.
He said, "Sweet Desdemona,
Let us be careful. Let us hide our love!"
Then he said, "Curse the fate that gave you to the Moor!"

OTHELLO: Oh, monstrous! Monstrous!

IAGO: Still, this was just his dream.

OTHELLO: It's very suspicious, even though it was only a dream.

IAGO: It might help to support other evidence.
Tell me, have you not sometimes seen a handkerchief
Decorated with strawberries in your wife's hand?

OTHELLO: Why? I gave her one like that.
It was my first gift to her.

IAGO: I didn't know that.
But I saw Cassio wipe his beard
With such a handkerchief today.

OTHELLO: If it's the same one—

IAGO: If it's the same one, or any one that is hers,
It speaks against her, along with the other proofs.

OTHELLO: Oh, I wish she had 40,000 lives!
One is too little, too small for my revenge!
Now I see that it is true.
All my dear love for her is gone.
Now you must help me.
Within three days, let me hear you say
That Cassio is no longer alive.

IAGO: He is as good as dead, by your request.
But let her live.

OTHELLO: Damn her, the wicked minx!
Oh, damn her! I must think of
Some swift means of death for the fair devil.
You are my lieutenant now.

IAGO: I am your servant forever.

(**Othello** and **Iago** exit.)

Scene 3 11

(Enter **Desdemona** and **Emilia** in front of the castle.)

DESDEMONA: Where could I have lost the handkerchief, Emilia?
I would rather have lost my purse full of gold coins!
If my noble Moor were not so sensible, this would be enough
To put evil thoughts in his head.

EMILIA: Isn't he jealous?

DESDEMONA: Who, Othello? Not in the least!

EMILIA: Look, here he comes.

(Enter **Othello**.)

DESDEMONA *(to Othello)***:** How are you, my lord?

OTHELLO: Well, my good lady.
(to himself): Oh, it is so hard to lie!
(to her): How are you, Desdemona?

DESDEMONA: Well, my lord. I have sent for Cassio to come speak with you.

OTHELLO: I have a terrible head cold. Lend me your handkerchief.

DESDEMONA: Here, my lord.

OTHELLO: I mean the one I gave you.

DESDEMONA: I don't have it with me.

OTHELLO: Is it lost? Is it gone? Tell me, have you left it somewhere?

DESDEMONA: It is not lost. But what if it were?

OTHELLO: Go get it. Let me see it.

DESDEMONA: Well, I could do that, sir, but I won't right now.
Now, I want to talk about Cassio.
Please give him his job back.

OTHELLO: Get me the handkerchief!

DESDEMONA: Come, come! You'll never find a more capable man.

OTHELLO: The handkerchief!

DESDEMONA: Please, let's talk about Cassio.

OTHELLO: The handkerchief !

DESDEMONA: Really, you have no reason to act this way.

OTHELLO: Get away from me! ***(Exit Othello.)***

EMILIA: And you say he isn't jealous?

DESDEMONA: I never saw him like this before!

EMILIA: Sometimes it takes years to see what a man is really like.

(Enter **Cassio** and **Iago**.)

Look, Cassio and my husband!

DESDEMONA: Cassio! What news have you?

CASSIO: Madam, the same as before.

I beg you to speak to your husband.

DESDEMONA: Oh, gentle Cassio! My words won't help right now.

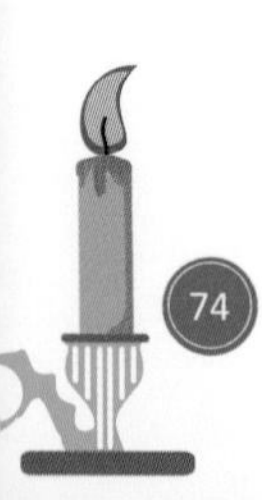

My lord is not himself. Be patient. I'll do what I can.

IAGO: Is my lord angry?

EMILIA: Yes, for some reason he seemed strangely disturbed. He left just now.

IAGO: How can he be angry? It must be something very serious.

I'll go see about it.

(Exit **Iago**.)

DESDEMONA *(calling after Iago)*: Please do.

(to Emilia): Some business of state must be bothering him.

I thought he was angry with me.

Now I realize it was something else.

EMILIA: Pray that state business concerns him rather than jealous thoughts.

DESDEMONA: I have never given him cause!

EMILIA: But jealous souls will not be answered that way.

They are never jealous for good reason, but only because they're jealous.

It is a monster that creates more of itself and was born of itself.

DESDEMONA: May heaven keep that monster from Othello's mind!

EMILIA: Amen to that, lady.

DESDEMONA: I'll look for him. Come, Emilia.

(Exit **Desdemona** and **Emilia**. Enter **Bianca**.)

BIANCA: Greetings, my friend Cassio. Why haven't you been to see me?

CASSIO: I was just coming to your house. Sweet Bianca, ***(giving her Desdemona's handkerchief)*** will you copy this embroidery for me?

BIANCA: Oh, Cassio, where did you get this?
Is it a gift from a new friend?
Now I know why you haven't been to see me lately. Well, well.

CASSIO: Go on, fair maid!
This isn't from another woman.

BIANCA: Well, whose is it?

CASSIO: I don't know, sweet. It was in my bedroom. I like the embroidery.
Before it is reclaimed, and I'm sure it will be, I'd like to have it copied.
Take it, and do it, and leave me alone awhile.

BIANCA: Leave you alone? Why?

CASSIO: I'm waiting for the general. I will see you soon.

BIANCA: All right. I'll look forward to it.

(Exit **Cassio** and **Bianca**.)

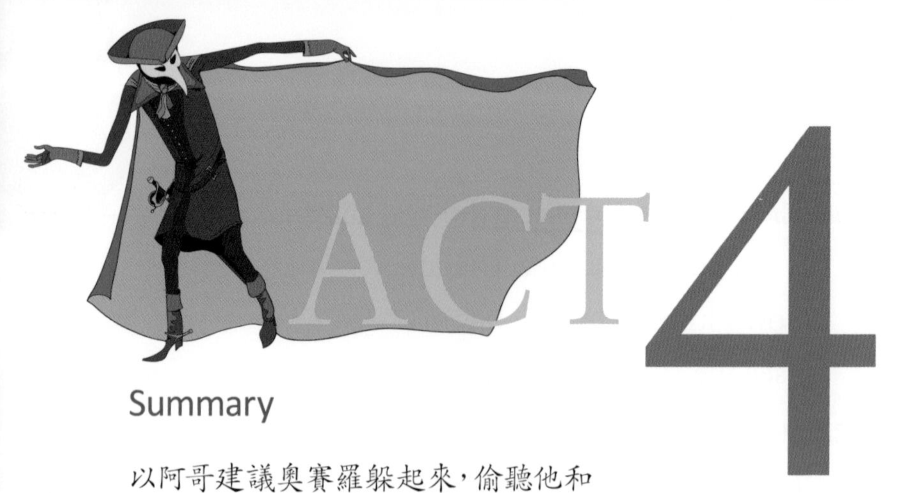

Summary

以阿哥建議奧賽羅躲起來，偷聽他和凱西奧聊天的內容。當凱西奧來找以阿哥時，以阿哥低聲提到畢昂嘉，在那之後，凱西奧用輕蔑的語氣來描述畢昂嘉，奧賽羅卻以為他是在說黛絲德夢娜。畢昂嘉生氣了，因為她發現那條手帕是屬於別的女人的。

當凱西奧和畢昂嘉離開後，奧賽羅誓言要因黛絲德夢娜對她不忠而置她於死地。公爵的代表從威尼斯捎了封信來，公爵希望奧賽羅能返回威尼斯，並讓凱西奧代理他在賽浦勒斯的職務。

奧賽羅當著黛絲德夢娜的面指控她不忠，而她聲淚俱下地否認。羅德里戈向以阿哥抱怨，即使他已將無數金銀財寶給以阿哥轉交給黛絲德夢娜，他仍然沒有跟黛絲德夢娜相處的機會。以阿哥告訴羅德里戈他必須殺死凱西奧，如此一來，奧賽羅和黛絲德夢娜則必須待在賽浦勒斯，這樣以阿哥才能繼續追求黛絲德夢娜。

黛絲德夢娜和艾米莉亞聊到對丈夫不忠的事，黛絲德夢娜說她絕對不會做這樣的事，即使「可以得到全世界」也不願意。

Scene 1 (12)

(Cyprus, in front of the castle: Enter **Othello** and **Iago**.)

IAGO: Do you think so?

OTHELLO: Think so, Iago?

IAGO: What, to kiss in private?

OTHELLO: An unauthorized kiss.

IAGO: Or to be naked with her friend in bed
An hour or more, not meaning any harm?

OTHELLO: Naked in bed, and not mean harm?
People who act that way will be tempted
By the devil, and they will tempt heaven.

IAGO: If they do nothing, it's a forgivable sin.
But if I give my wife a handkerchief—

OTHELLO: What then?

IAGO: Why, then, it's hers, my lord. As hers,
She may, I think, give it to any man.

OTHELLO: Her honor belongs to her, too.
May she give that away?

IAGO: Her honor is a quality that's not seen.
Some seem to have it when they don't.
But, as for the handkerchief—

OTHELLO: I wish I had forgotten it!
But now I remember that he had it.

IAGO: Yes, what of it?

OTHELLO: That's not so good.

IAGO: What if I said I saw him do you wrong?
Or if I had heard him blab—

OTHELLO: What has he said?

IAGO: Why, that he did—I don't know—lie—

OTHELLO: With her?

IAGO: With her, on her—what you will.

OTHELLO: Lie with her? Lie on her? By God, that's disgusting! Is this possible? Oh, devil!

(He falls into a trance.)

IAGO *(aside)***:** My medicine is working!
This is how gullible fools are caught,
And how many worthy and chaste women,
All innocent, wind up accused.

(Enter **Cassio**.)

CASSIO: What happened?

IAGO: My lord has had an epileptic seizure.
Look, he's stirring now.

Step out of the way for a while.
When he recovers and leaves,
I need to talk to you. It's very important.

(Exit **Cassio**.)

IAGO ***(to Othello)*****:** How are you, General?

OTHELLO: Not well. Did he confess it?

IAGO: Good sir, take it like a man.
You're not the first man it's happened to.
Better to know the truth, don't you think?

OTHELLO: Oh, you are wise! That's certain.

IAGO: Step aside for a while.
While you were out, Cassio came by.
I made him leave, but he promised to
return later.
Why don't you hide yourself,
And observe with your own eyes
The sneers and the scorn on his face?
I will make him tell the story again
Of where, how often, and when
He has—and will again—meet your wife.
I tell you, just watch how he acts.

OTHELLO: Thank you, Iago. ***(Othello hides.)***

IAGO ***(to himself)*****:** I'll ask Cassio about Bianca.
She's a hussy who sells herself to him
To buy herself bread and clothes.
She loves Cassio. It's typical of whores
To attract many men, but love only one.
When a man hears of her love,
He can't help but laugh. Here is Cassio.

(Enter **Cassio**.)

When he smiles, Othello shall go mad.
(to Cassio): How are you, Lieutenant?

CASSIO: All the worse since you call me by that title, the lack of which is killing me.

IAGO: Work on Desdemona, and you're sure to get it back.
(speaking lower): Now, if Bianca had anything to do with it,
How quickly you'd have your job back!

CASSIO: Yes, that poor fool loves me!

OTHELLO: Look how he laughs already!

IAGO: I never knew a woman so in love!

CASSIO: The pitiful wretch!

IAGO: Haven't you heard? She's saying
That you're going to marry her.
Do you really intend to?

CASSIO: Ha, ha, ha! Marry her—a prostitute?
Please give me more credit than that!
Ha, ha, ha!
She was just here. She follows me around.
I must get rid of her.

IAGO *(in a low voice)*: Well, look! Here she is.

(Enter **Bianca**.)

CASSIO *(to Bianca)*: Are you following me?

BIANCA: Let the devil and his mother follow you! What did you mean by giving me that handkerchief? I was a fine fool to take it! You say you found it in your bedroom and don't know who left it there? Some hussy, no doubt. Here! Give it back to your whore. I'm not copying the embroidery.

CASSIO: What's this, my sweet Bianca?

OTHELLO: By heaven, that's my handkerchief!

BIANCA: If you want to come to supper tonight, you may. If you don't, only come back again when you're invited.

(Exit **Bianca**.)

CASSIO: I'd better go after her. Otherwise, she'll be yelling in the streets about me.

IAGO: Will you have supper there?

CASSIO: Yes, I intend to.

IAGO: Well, I might see you later. I really need to speak with you.

CASSIO: I'll see you later, then.

(Exit **Cassio**.)

OTHELLO *(coming forward)*: I'll kill him, Iago!

IAGO: Did you see how he laughed at his sin? And did you see the handkerchief?

OTHELLO: I could spend nine years killing him. A fine woman! A lovely woman!

IAGO: No, you must forget all that.

OTHELLO: Yes, let her rot and perish and be damned tonight, for she shall not live! No, my heart is turned to stone. Oh,

but that sweet creature could sing the savageness right out of a bear! She has such a gentle way about her!

IAGO: Yes, too gentle.

OTHELLO: That's certain now. But yet the pity of it, Iago! Oh, Iago, the pity of it!

IAGO: If you care about her that much,
Why don't you just look the other way?
If it doesn't bother you, it won't bother anyone.

OTHELLO: I will chop her into little bits! She made a fool of me—with my officer!

IAGO: That's even worse.

OTHELLO: Get me some poison, Iago. Tonight!

IAGO: Don't use poison. Strangle her in her bed, the very bed she has contaminated.

OTHELLO: Good, good! The justice of that pleases me. Very good!

IAGO: As for Cassio, let me take care of him. You shall hear more by midnight.

(A trumpet blows offstage. Enter **Lodovico**, **Desdemona**, and **attendants**.)

OTHELLO: What was that trumpet?

IAGO: Surely someone from Venice. It's Lodovico. He's come from the duke. Look, your wife is with him.

LODOVICO: The duke and senators of Venice greet you. ***(He gives Othello a letter.)***

OTHELLO: I kiss this letter. ***(He opens the letter and reads it.)***

LODOVICO: How's Lieutenant Cassio doing?

IAGO: He lives, sir.

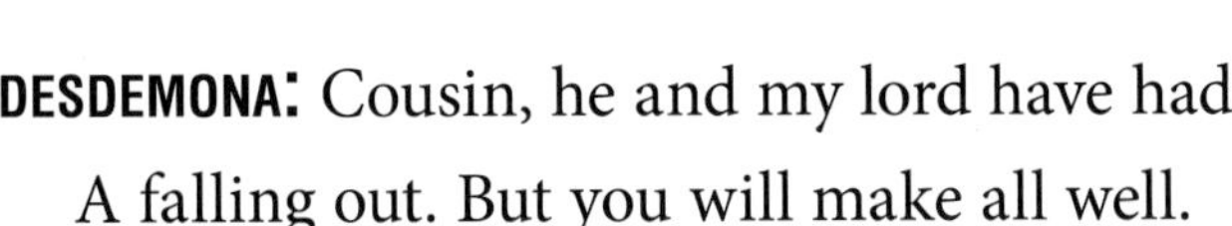

DESDEMONA: Cousin, he and my lord have had
A falling out. But you will make all well.

OTHELLO: Are you sure of that?

DESDEMONA: My lord?

OTHELLO ***(reading):*** "Do it as soon as you can—"

LODOVICO: He wasn't speaking to you. He's
busy with his letter.
Is there trouble between my lord and Cassio?

DESDEMONA: Very bad trouble. I want them
To make up, for the love I feel for Cassio.

OTHELLO: Fire and brimstone!

DESDEMONA: My lord?

LODOVICO: Maybe the letter has upset him.
I think they want him to go home
And leave his position here to Cassio.

DESDEMONA: Well, really, I'm glad to hear it.

OTHELLO ***(striking her):*** Devil!

DESDEMONA ***(shocked and horrified):*** I've done
nothing to deserve this.

LODOVICO: My lord, no one would believe this
in Venice, even if I swore I saw it.
Apologize to her. She's weeping.

OTHELLO: Oh, devil, devil!
If the earth were sown by woman's tears,
Her tears would become crocodiles!
Out of my sight!

DESDEMONA: I will not stay to offend you.

(Weak with shock, she turns to go.)

OTHELLO: Go away! I'll send for you soon.

(Exit **Desdemona**, crying bitterly.)

(to Lodovico, furiously): Sir, I'll obey this letter and return to Venice.
Cassio shall have my place! And, sir,
Tonight I hope we can dine together.
You are welcome to Cyprus.

(He bows, then leaves in a trembling rage.)

Goats and monkeys!

LODOVICO: Is this the noble Moor whom our senate thought to be so capable?
The man whom anger could not shake?

IAGO: He is much changed.

LODOVICO: Is his mind all right? Is he mad?

IAGO: He's what he seems to be. I wish
He could be what he might have been!

LODOVICO: And he struck his wife?

IAGO: Alas! That was not so good.
And I'm afraid he might do worse.

LODOVICO: Is he usually like this?
Or did the letter make him angry?

IAGO: Alas, alas! I should not speak about
What I have seen. Watch him yourself.

LODOVICO: I'm sorry I was wrong about him.

(**All** exit.)

Scene 2 13

(A room in the castle. Enter **Othello** and **Emilia**.)

OTHELLO: You have seen nothing, then?

EMILIA: Nor ever heard or suspected anything.

OTHELLO: But you have seen her with Cassio?

EMILIA: Yes, but I saw no harm in it.
I heard everything they said to each other.

OTHELLO: What—they didn't even whisper?

EMILIA: Never, my lord.

OTHELLO: Nor send you out of the way?

EMILIA: Never!

OTHELLO: That's strange.

EMILIA: My lord, I would bet my soul that she is faithful.
Never think otherwise!
If some villain has given you this idea,
Let heaven punish him.
If she isn't faithful, chaste, and true,
There's not a happy man in the world.

OTHELLO: Tell her to come to me. Go.

(Exit **Emilia**.)

Her words sound good. Yet any stupid
Woman could make up such a story.

(Enter **Desdemona** and **Emilia**.)

DESDEMONA: My lord, what do you wish?

OTHELLO: Let me see your eyes. Look at me.

DESDEMONA: What horrible ideas do you have?

OTHELLO *(to Emilia)*: Leave us alone and shut the door.

(Exit **Emilia**.)

OTHELLO: Tell me, what are you?

DESDEMONA: Your wife, my lord.
Your true and loyal wife.

OTHELLO: Come, swear you are honest.

DESDEMONA: Heaven truly knows I am!

OTHELLO: Heaven knows you are false as hell.

DESDEMONA: What? To whom, my lord?
With whom? How am I false?

OTHELLO: Ah, Desdemona! Get away! Away!

DESDEMONA: Oh, what a sad day!
Why do you weep?

Am I the cause of these tears, my lord?
Do you suspect my father for having you
called back to Venice?
Don't blame me for it.

OTHELLO: If heaven had sent me some illness,
Or buried me in poverty up to my lips,
Or made me a slave, I could have taken it.
But to be driven from the place
Where I have gathered up my heart—
This makes me grim as hell!

DESDEMONA: My noble lord,
I pray you know that I am faithful.

OTHELLO: I wish you'd never been born!

DESDEMONA: Alas! What sin have I
unknowingly committed?

OTHELLO: What sin have you committed?
You impudent harlot!

DESDEMONA: By God, you do me wrong.

OTHELLO: Are you not a harlot?

DESDEMONA: No, I swear to you as a Christian!

OTHELLO: What—you're not a whore?

DESDEMONA: No! I swear it by heaven.

OTHELLO: Is it possible?

DESDEMONA: Oh, heaven help us!

OTHELLO: I ask your pardon, then.
I thought you were that sly whore of
Venice who married Othello.
(shouting): Come here, woman!

(Enter **Emilia**.)

You who have the opposite job of St. Peter
And keep the gate of hell! You, yes, you!
(giving her money): We are finished. Here's
money for your trouble.
Please, keep this meeting secret.

(Exit **Othello**.)

EMILIA: My God, what is he thinking?
Are you all right, my good lady?

DESDEMONA: Really, I'm in shock.
I cannot weep, and I can't say anything
That shouldn't be said with tears.
Make up my bed with my wedding sheets.
And call your husband here.

EMILIA: Things are certainly changed!

(Exit **Emilia**.)

DESDEMONA: Heaven pity me! What have I done to make him think me unfaithful?

(Enter **Iago** and **Emilia**.)

IAGO: What can I do for you, madam?

DESDEMONA: I don't know exactly.

IAGO: What's the matter, lady?

EMILIA: Alas, Iago, my lord has cruelly called her a whore.

IAGO: Why did he do this?

DESDEMONA: I don't know.

IAGO: Do not weep! What a sad day!

EMILIA: Has she refused so many noble matches,
Her father, her country, and her friends,
To be called a whore?
Doesn't she have a right to weep?

IAGO: Curse him for it! Why did he say this?

DESDEMONA: Only heaven knows.

EMILIA: Some villain, some cheating scoundrel
Must have told this lie to get ahead.
You can hang me if I'm wrong.

IAGO: There is no such man. It's impossible.

DESDEMONA: If there is, heaven forgive him!

EMILIA: May a noose forgive him!
And may hell gnaw on his bones!
Why should anyone call her a whore?
The Moor has been misled by a villain.

IAGO: Watch what you say.

EMILIA: Oh, to hell with him!
It was just that kind of man who
Made you think I was the Moor's lover!

IAGO: You are a fool. Watch yourself.

DESDEMONA: Iago, good friend, talk to him.
I tell you, I love him dearly.
His unkindness may destroy my life,
But it will never change my love.

IAGO: Don't be upset. It's just his mood.
Business of state has made him angry,
And he takes it out on you.
That's all it is, I assure you.

(Trumpets blow offstage.)

Listen, the trumpets call you to supper!
Go in, and stop crying. All will be fine.

(Exit **Desdemona** and **Emilia**. Enter **Roderigo**.)

Greetings, Roderigo!

RODERIGO: You've been cheating me, sir.

IAGO: In what way?

RODERIGO: You keep putting me off, Iago. I have wasted all my money. The jewels I've given you to give to Desdemona would have half-corrupted a nun. You've said that she's received them. You've led me to have hopes of getting closer to her. But it hasn't happened.

IAGO: Well, calm down. All is well.

RODERIGO: No, all is not well! In fact, I'm starting to feel you can't be trusted. I will make myself known to Desdemona. If

she will return my jewels to me, I will leave her alone. If not, be certain that I'll make you pay.

IAGO: Well, now I see you've got some backbone. You have good cause for your anger! Still, I assure you, I have been very fair with you.

RODERIGO: It doesn't appear that way.

IAGO: I admit that. Your suspicions are not foolish. But Roderigo, I'm convinced more than ever that you have determination, courage, and valor. Show it tonight! If Desdemona isn't yours tomorrow night, take me from this world with treachery!

RODERIGO: Well, what is your plan? Is it reasonable and possible?

IAGO: Sir, an official order came from Venice. Cassio is to take Othello's place.

RODERIGO: Is that true? Why, then, Othello and Desdemona will return to Venice.

IAGO: Oh, no. He'll go to Mauritania, taking Desdemona, unless some accident forces

him to stay here. Getting rid of Cassio would simply be the accident to force that result.

RODERIGO: Getting rid of him? What do you mean?

IAGO: Why, by making him unable to take Othello's place—by knocking out his brains.

RODERIGO: That's what you want me to do?

IAGO: Yes—if you dare do the best thing for yourself. Cassio is eating with a harlot tonight. I'm going to meet him there. He doesn't know the news of his good fortune yet. If you watch for him to leave, you can finish him off at your leisure. I'll be nearby to back you up. Between the two of us, he'll die. Don't look so shocked, but come with me.

RODERIGO: I want to hear more reasons for this.

IAGO: You'll hear them!

(**Roderigo** and **Iago** exit.)

Scene 3 14

(Another room in the castle: Enter **Othello**, **Lodovico**, **Desdemona**, **Emilia**, and **attendants**.)

OTHELLO *(to Lodovico)*: Walk with me, sir?
(to Desdemona): Go to bed at once. I'll return soon. Send your servant away now. Be sure to do it.

DESDEMONA: I will, my lord.

(Exit **Othello**, **Lodovico**, and **attendants**.)

EMILIA: He seems to be in a better mood.

DESDEMONA: He says he'll be back soon.
He told me to go to bed
And to send you away.

EMILIA: What? Send me away?

DESDEMONA: That was his wish. So, Emilia,
Give me my night clothes, and goodbye.
We must not displease him now.

EMILIA: I wish you had never met him!

DESDEMONA: But I don't. I love him truly.

EMILIA ***(helping her change for bed)*****:** I've put those sheets you asked for on the bed.

DESDEMONA: It doesn't matter. My goodness, how foolish we are!
If I die before you, please wrap me
In one of these same sheets.

EMILIA: Come now! What kind of talk is that?

DESDEMONA: Oh, these men! These men!
Do you honestly think—tell me, Emilia—
That there are women who are unfaithful
To their husbands?

EMILIA: There are some. No question about it.

DESDEMONA: Would you do such a deed for all the world?

EMILIA: Why—wouldn't you?

DESDEMONA: No, I swear by the light of all the stars that I wouldn't!

EMILIA: Well, I wouldn't do it by the light of the stars.
It would be easier to do in the dark.

DESDEMONA: Would you truly do such a deed for all the world?

EMILIA: The world's a huge thing.
It would be a great payment
For a small sin.

DESDEMONA: Surely you don't mean that!

EMILIA: I do. I'd make up for it once it was done. Of course, I wouldn't do such a thing for a little ring, or for property, nor for dresses, gowns, or caps, or any small gift. But for the whole world? For God's sake! Who wouldn't be unfaithful to her husband to make him a king?

DESDEMONA: Curse me if I would do such a wrong
Even for the whole world!

EMILIA: Why, that wrong is just one of many in the world! And if you'd get the whole

world for your trouble, then it's wrong in your own world. You could quickly make everything right again.

DESDEMONA: I do not think there is any such woman!

EMILIA: There are enough to fill the world!
But I do think it is their husbands' faults
When wives do wrong. Suppose they
Give our valuables to other women,
Or else have a fit of foolish jealousy
And keep us from coming and going.
Or suppose they strike us—
Why, we can become resentful, too!
We can even become vengeful.
Wives have feelings just like husbands.
They see, smell, and have tastes
For both sweet and sour things
Just as their husbands do. Why do they
Reject us for other women? Is it for sport?
I think it is. And does it result from desire?
I think so. Does frailty lead them to sin?
It certainly does. And don't we have

longings, desires, and frailty, just as our men do?
Let them treat us well—or let them know
We will behave just as they do, just so.

DESDEMONA: Good night, good night.
May heaven teach me
Not to return evil with evil, but to learn from it!

(Exit **Desdemona** and **Emilia**.)

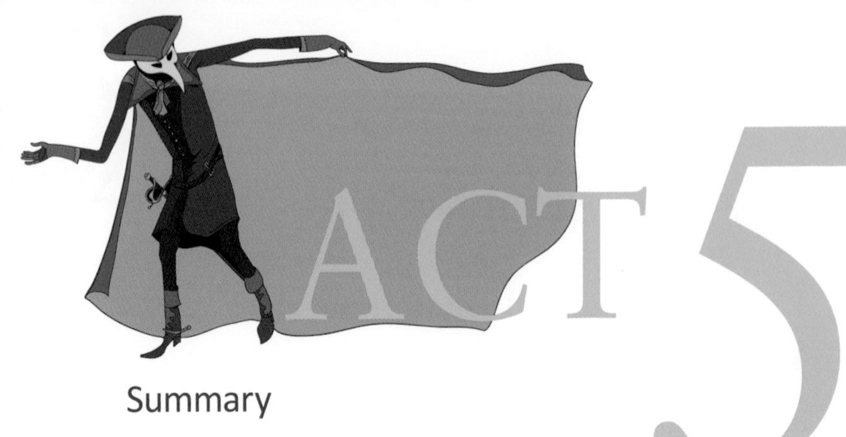

Summary

邪惡的以阿哥想置凱西奧和羅德里戈於死地。如此一來，凱西奧就無法揭露以阿哥的謊言，而他也可以私吞羅德里戈給黛絲德夢娜的所有禮物。凱西奧和羅德里戈在一場對戰中傷了彼此，而以阿哥暗中刺傷兩人，殺了羅德里戈。

奧賽羅指責黛絲德夢娜出軌，並將她悶死。艾米莉亞進門，說羅德里戈已被倖存的凱西奧所殺。黛絲德夢娜奄奄一息，對艾米莉亞交代遺言，她沒有責怪奧賽羅將她殺死。奧賽羅承認他殺了她，說他從以阿哥那裡得到黛絲德夢娜出軌的證據。艾米莉亞大喊尋求幫忙，而以阿哥和其他人進門。

當奧賽羅舉出手帕當作出軌證據，艾米莉亞說出實情，以阿哥刺殺艾米莉亞後逃跑。有些人上前去追以阿哥，留奧賽羅和垂死的艾米莉亞獨留一室。她告訴奧賽羅，黛絲德夢娜很愛他，一向守身如玉。當以阿哥被抓時，他跟凱西奧被帶回奧賽羅家。奧賽羅刺殺以阿哥卻沒成功，旋即用刀自戕。凱西奧接管賽浦勒斯，並誓言讓以阿哥受到懲罰。

Scene 1 (15)

(A street in Cyprus: Enter **Iago** and **Roderigo**.)

IAGO: He'll be coming by soon, Roderigo.
Keep your sword out. Be ready to use it.
Quick, quick! Fear nothing. I'll be near.

RODERIGO: Stay close. I might make a mistake.

IAGO: I am right here. Be bold!

(**Iago** hides himself.)

RODERIGO: I'm not sure about this.
But he has given me good reasons for it.
It will be just another man dead.
My sword is ready! He'll die!

IAGO *(aside)*: Very good. I've rubbed this
young pimple almost raw,
And now he's getting angry.
Whether he kills Cassio, or Cassio him,
Or they kill each other, it will all
Be good for me. If Roderigo lives,
He'll want me to give back all the
Gold and jewels that I swindled from him
As gifts for Desdemona.

That must not happen. If Cassio survives,
The Moor might reveal my lies to him.
That would be very dangerous for me—
So he must die! I hear him coming.

(Enter **Cassio**.)

RODERIGO: I know his walk. It's Cassio!
Villain, prepare to die!

(Roderigo attacks Cassio with a sword, but does no damage. Cassio draws his own sword and wounds Roderigo seriously.)

RODERIGO: Oh, I've been killed!

(**Iago** wounds Cassio's leg and quickly exits.)

CASSIO: I've been maimed! Help! Murder!
Murder! *(He falls.)*

(Enter **Othello**.)

OTHELLO *(to himself)***:** That's Cassio!
Iago kept his word. Oh, brave Iago!
How strongly he feels for a friend who's been wronged.
He teaches me! So now, hussy, your lover lies dead,
And your own death is near. I'm coming, harlot.

Your charms are blotted out of my heart,
And your lust-stained bed shall soon be
stained with your lustful blood.

(Exit **Othello**. Enter **Lodovico** and **Gratiano**.)

CASSIO: Help! No passers-by? Murder!

GRATIANO: What a frightening cry!

CASSIO: Oh, help!

LODOVICO: Listen! It's so dark, I can't see.

RODERIGO: Oh, wretched villain! Won't anybody help? Then I shall bleed to death.

(Enter **Iago**, carrying a light.)

IAGO: Did I hear a cry?

CASSIO: Here, here! For heaven's sake, help!

IAGO: What's the matter?

CASSIO: Iago? Over here! I have been injured by villains!

IAGO: Oh, no, Lieutenant! Who has done this?

CASSIO: I think one of them is nearby
And cannot get away.

IAGO: Oh, the treacherous villains!
(to Lodovico and Gratiano): Who's over there? Come and give me some help.

RODERIGO: Oh, help me here!

CASSIO: That's one of them.

IAGO *(to Roderigo)*: You murderous scum! You villain! ***(Iago stabs Roderigo.)***

RODERIGO: Oh, damned Iago! You inhuman dog! ***(Roderigo dies.)***

IAGO: The idea of killing men in the dark!
Where are these bloodthirsty thieves?
This town is so silent! Ho! Murder!
Murder! ***(to Lodovico and Gratiano)***: Who are you? Are you good or evil?

LODOVICO: Judge us by our actions.

IAGO: Signior Lodovico?

LODOVICO: Yes, sir.

IAGO: I beg your pardon. Here's Cassio, who's been attacked by villains.

GRATIANO: Cassio!

IAGO: How are you, brother?

CASSIO: My leg has been cut deeply.

IAGO: I'll bandage it with my shirt.

(Enter **Bianca**.)

BIANCA ***(seeing Cassio)*****:** Oh, Cassio!
My dear Cassio! Oh, Cassio, Cassio!

IAGO: Gentlemen all, I suspect this slut
Had something to do with this injury.
(holding a light over Roderigo): Do we know this man, or not?
Alas, it is my dear friend Roderigo!
It can't be. Yet it is. Heavens! Roderigo!
(to Cassio): What malice was between you?

CASSIO: None. I don't even know him.

IAGO ***(to Bianca)*****:** Why, you look very pale.
The terror in your eyes hints at guilt.
(to the others): Carry them away. I will send a doctor for Cassio.

(**Cassio** and **Roderigo** are carried off. Enter **Emilia**.)

EMILIA: What's the matter, husband?

IAGO: Cassio was attacked here in the dark
By Roderigo and others who escaped.
He was almost killed. Roderigo is dead.

EMILIA: Oh, alas, good Cassio!

IAGO: This is what comes of whoring.
Please, Emilia, go ask Cassio where he had supper tonight.
(to Bianca): What? Does my question make you shake?

BIANCA: He had supper at my house—but I'm not shaking because of that.

IAGO: Oh, he did? I order you, come with me.

EMILIA: Curses on you, harlot!

BIANCA: I am no harlot. I am as honest as any of my accusers.

EMILIA: Nonsense! Curses on you!

IAGO: Let's get a doctor for Cassio.
(to Bianca): Come along, woman. You'd better come up with another story.
Emilia, run to the castle
And tell my lord and lady what has happened. Hurry!

(**They** exit.)

Scene 2

(**Desdemona** is sleeping in a bedchamber in the castle. Enter **Othello** with a candle.)

OTHELLO: I'll not shed her blood nor scar
Her skin, which is whiter than snow.
Yet she must die, or she'll betray more men.
I'll put out this light, and then put out her light. ***(He kisses her.)***
Her sweet breath almost persuades me to spare her.
One more kiss, one more! This is the last!
Such sweetness was never before so fatal.
I must weep, but they are cruel tears.
My sorrow is like God's when he punishes
His beloved sinners. She's waking up.

DESDEMONA: Who's there? Othello?

OTHELLO: Yes, Desdemona.

DESDEMONA: Will you come to bed, my lord?

OTHELLO: Have you prayed tonight?

DESDEMONA: Yes, my lord.

OTHELLO: Can you think of any sin
That you haven't yet confessed to heaven?
If so, ask forgiveness now.
I don't want to kill your unprepared spirit.

DESDEMONA: What? Do you talk of killing?

OTHELLO: Yes, I do.

DESDEMONA: Then heaven have mercy on me!

OTHELLO: Think about your sins.

DESDEMONA: They are all the different loves
I have for you.

OTHELLO: Yes, and for that you will die.

DESDEMONA: It's unnatural to kill out of love.
What's the matter?

OTHELLO: That handkerchief that I gave
to you—
You gave it to Cassio.

DESDEMONA: No, I swear by my life and soul!
I never wronged you in my life!
I love Cassio only as a friend.
I never gave him a token of love.

OTHELLO: I saw my handkerchief in his hand,
You lying woman!

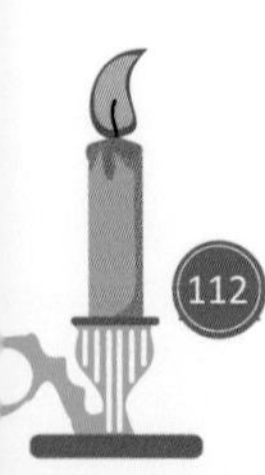

You have turned my heart into stone.
You make me call what I intend to do
A murder, when I meant it as a sacrifice.
I saw the handkerchief!

DESDEMONA: He must have found it, then.
I never gave it to him. Send for him.
Let him confess the truth.

OTHELLO: He has confessed.

DESDEMONA: To what, my lord?

OTHELLO: That he has used you.

DESDEMONA: How? Improperly?

OTHELLO: Yes.

DESDEMONA: He wouldn't say that.

OTHELLO: No, his mouth has been stopped.
I ordered honest Iago to see to it.

DESDEMONA: What—is he dead?

OTHELLO: If all his hairs had been lives, my revenge would have killed them all.

DESDEMONA: Alas! He has been betrayed, and I am finished!

OTHELLO: Enough, harlot! Are you weeping for him to my face?

DESDEMONA: Oh, banish me, my lord, but do not kill me!

OTHELLO: Down with you, harlot!

DESDEMONA: But let me say one prayer!

OTHELLO: It is too late!

(Othello smothers Desdemona.)

EMILIA ***(outside the door)*****:** My lord, my lord!

OTHELLO ***(still smothering Desdemona, as she struggles)*****:**
What is this noise? Not quite dead?
I may be cruel, but I'm also merciful.

I would not have you linger in your pain.
There, there.

EMILIA ***(from offstage)*:** My lord, my lord! I need to talk to you!

OTHELLO ***(to Emilia)*:** Yes, yes, just a minute!
(to himself): It's Emilia. She's probably come to tell me of Cassio's death.
(looking at Desdemona): No more movement?
Still as the grave. Shall I let the maid in? Is that wise?
I think she stirs again. What's best to do?
If the maid comes in, she'll want to speak to my wife.
My wife! What wife? I have no wife!
Oh, this is unbearable! Oh, heavy hour!

EMILIA: Let me talk with you, my lord!

OTHELLO: I'll be right there! ***(to himself)***: I'll pull the curtains closed around the bed.
(opening the door): What's the matter?

EMILIA: Oh, my good lord, a foul murder has been done!
Cassio has killed a young Venetian named Roderigo.

OTHELLO: Roderigo's been killed? And Cassio?

EMILIA: No, Cassio's not been killed.

OTHELLO: Cassio's not been killed? Then the wrong murder has been committed
And my sweet revenge has turned bitter.

DESDEMONA ***(weakly)*****:** Wrongly, wrongly murdered!

EMILIA: Oh, lord, what is that voice?

OTHELLO: That? What?

EMILIA: Oh, no! That was my lady's voice.
(pulling back the bed curtains): Help! Help!
Oh, lady, speak again! Sweet Desdemona!
Oh, sweet mistress, speak!

DESDEMONA: A guiltless death I die.

EMILIA: Oh, who has done this deed?

DESDEMONA: Nobody. I, myself. Goodbye.
Speak well of me to my kind lord.
Oh, farewell! ***(She dies.)***

OTHELLO: It was I who killed her.

EMILIA: Oh, then she's all the more an angel,
And you're an even blacker devil!

OTHELLO: She was unfaithful to me. She was
a whore.

EMILIA: You are slandering her, you devil!
She was as true as heaven!

OTHELLO: Cassio made love to her.
Your husband knew all about it.

EMILIA: My husband?

OTHELLO: Your husband.

EMILIA: That she broke her marriage vows?

OTHELLO: Yes, with Cassio.

EMILIA: My husband!

OTHELLO: Why do you repeat yourself, woman?
I said your husband.
My friend, your husband, honest Iago.

EMILIA: If he said so, may his evil soul
Rot little by little! He's lying.
She was too fond of her filthy marriage.
This deed you've done is no more worthy
of heaven
Than you were worthy of her.

OTHELLO: Ha! You'd better be quiet.

EMILIA: You fool! You dolt! You are
As ignorant as dirt! I'll turn you in
Even if you kill me twenty times.
Help! Help! Somebody, help!
The Moor has killed my lady! Murder!

(Enter **Montano**, **Gratiano**, **Iago**, and **others**.)

MONTANO: What's the matter?

EMILIA: Oh, you've come, too, Iago?
You've done well, to have other men
Blame their murders on you.
Prove this villain wrong—if you're a man.
He says you told him his wife was false.
I know you didn't. You are not that evil.
Speak, for my heart is in anguish.

IAGO: I told him what I suspected.
It was what he found to be true.

EMILIA: But did you ever say she was false?

IAGO: I did.

EMILIA: You told a lie, a foul, damned lie!
She—with Cassio? Did you say Cassio?

IAGO: With Cassio, woman. Calm down.

EMILIA: I will not calm down. I must speak!
My lady lies here, murdered in her bed—

ALL: Oh, heaven forbid!

EMILIA: And your words, Iago, have brought about this murder.

OTHELLO: Stop staring, gentlemen. It is true.

GRATIANO: This is terrible!

MONTANO: A monstrous act!

EMILIA: Villainy, villainy, villainy!
I'll kill myself out of grief!

IAGO: Are you mad? I order you to go home.

EMILIA: Perhaps, Iago, I will never go home.

OTHELLO: Oh! Oh! Oh! ***(He falls on the bed.)***

EMILIA: Go right ahead and lie there roaring!
For you have killed the sweetest innocent
That ever lived.

OTHELLO *(rising)*: Oh, she was wicked!
It's a pity, but still, Iago knows that
She and Cassio committed the act of shame a thousand times.
And she rewarded these foul acts
With a pledge of love that I first gave her.
I saw the handkerchief in his hand—
An old gift my father gave my mother.

EMILIA: Oh, God! Oh, heavenly God!

IAGO: By God, keep quiet!

EMILIA: I'll speak as freely as the north wind.
Oh, you stupid Moor! That handkerchief
I found only by chance and gave it to
my husband,
For often, with solemn earnestness
He begged me to steal it.

IAGO: You villainous whore!

EMILIA: Did she give it to Cassio? No.
I found it—and I gave it to my husband.

IAGO: You filthy thing, you lie!

EMILIA: By heaven, I do not, gentlemen.
(to Othello): You murderous idiot!
Why did such a fool have so good a wife?

(Othello attacks Iago but is stopped by Montano. Iago stabs Emilia with his sword.)

GRATIANO: He has killed his wife.

EMILIA: Yes, yes. Lay me by my lady's side.

(Exit **Iago**.)

GRATIANO: He's gone, but his wife is killed.

MONTANO: What a villain! Use this weapon
Which I have just taken from the Moor
To guard the outside door. Kill him if
He tries to leave. I'll go after Iago,
For he is a damned scoundrel.

(Exit **Montano** and **Gratiano**, leaving **Othello** and **Emilia** alone.)

OTHELLO: I seem to have lost my courage.
Now any weakling can take my sword!
But why should my honor outlive me?
Let me lose everything.

EMILIA: Moor, she was chaste.
She loved you, cruel Moor.
I speak the truth—and I die. ***(She dies.)***

OTHELLO: I have another sword in this room.
Oh, here it is. ***(calling outside)***: Uncle, I must come out!

GRATIANO *(from offstage)*: If you try it, it will cost you dearly.
You have no weapon, and would lose.

OTHELLO: Come in, then, and speak with me,
Or I'll attack, even though I'm unarmed.

(Enter **Gratiano**.)

GRATIANO: What is the matter?

OTHELLO: Look, I do have a weapon.
Don't be afraid. This is my journey's end.
(to Desdemona): How do you look now?
Oh, ill-fated woman! Pale as your gown!
Cold, cold, my girl! Just like your virtue.
Oh, what a cursed fool I am!
Whip me, you devils.
Take this heavenly sight from my mind!
Wash me in gulfs of liquid fire!
O Desdemona! Dead, Desdemona! Dead!
Oh! Oh! Oh!

(Enter **Lodovico**, **Montano**, **Cassio** carried in a chair, and Officer, with Iago as a prisoner.)

LODOVICO: Where is this unfortunate man?

OTHELLO: He who was once Othello? Here.
(to Iago): You devil! ***(He stabs Iago.)***

LODOVICO: Get the sword away from him!

(Othello is disarmed.)

IAGO: I'm bleeding, sir, but not killed.

OTHELLO: I am not sorry. I'd rather you live,
For, to my mind, it's happiness to die.

LODOVICO: Did you and he plot to kill Cassio?

OTHELLO: Yes.

CASSIO: Dear General, I gave you no cause.

OTHELLO: I believe you, and I ask your pardon!
Ask Iago why he trapped me into this.

IAGO: Ask me nothing. I won't speak again.

OTHELLO *(to Iago)*: You hateful coward.
Cassio, how did you get that handkerchief
That was my wife's?

CASSIO: I found it in my room. Iago confessed
That he left it there on purpose
In order to carry out his plan.

OTHELLO: Oh, I am a fool! A fool! A fool!

CASSIO: We found a letter written by
Roderigo.
He accuses Iago of making him

Bait me when I was on watch,
Which led to my dismissal.
So even now he speaks,
Long after his death. Iago ruined him.
Iago led him on.

LODOVICO *(to Othello)*: Come with us.
Your power and your command are taken.
Cassio now rules in Cyprus. As for Iago—
If any torture can torment him greatly,
It shall be used against him.
You shall be kept a close prisoner
Until the nature of your crimes is known
To the Venetian state. Come, let's go.

OTHELLO: Wait! A word or two before you go.
I beg you, when you tell of this, speak
Of one that loved not wisely but too well.
Of one not easily jealous, but being
Disturbed, grew extremely confused.
Of one whose hand threw a pearl away
Worth more than all his people.
Write all this! Also say that once,
When a vicious Turk in a turban
Attacked a Venetian and insulted the state,

I took the dog by the throat
And killed him—like this. ***(Stabs himself with a knife he had hidden.)***

LODOVICO: Oh, what a bloody end!

OTHELLO ***(to Desdemona)*****:** I kissed you before I killed you.
Now there is no way but this,
Killing myself, to die with a kiss.

(Falls on the bed, kisses her, and dies.)

LODOVICO ***(to Iago)*****:** Oh, Spartan dog!
Look at the tragic victims on this bed.
This is your work. The sight is horrible.
Let it be hidden.
(to Gratiano): Gratiano, guard the house
And take the Moor's property,
Since you are the heir.
(to Cassio): Lord Governor, it is your duty
To see that this hellish villain is punished.
I'll leave at once and, with a heavy heart, report to the state
These sad acts.

(**All** exit.)

中文翻譯

簡介

英文內文 P. 004

這部劇作的背景是在義大利威尼斯，以及地中海的賽浦勒斯島，時間是一六〇〇年代初期。奧賽羅是個來自北非的摩爾人，也是偉大的威尼斯軍事將領。在本劇開始之初，奧賽羅的旗官以阿哥未被列入晉升之列；相反地，奧賽羅提拔了年紀較輕的凱西奧。以阿哥非常生氣；為了報復，他計畫利用奧賽羅的善妒，離間奧賽羅與他的新婚妻子黛絲德夢娜。隨著劇情的發展，這位尊貴的摩爾人落入了以阿哥的陷阱中，悲劇隨之發生。

人物介紹

P. 005

列威尼斯公爵

柏拉班修：黛絲德夢娜的父親，元老

葛拉提安諾：柏拉班修的弟弟，威尼斯貴族

羅多維柯：柏拉班修的親戚，威尼斯貴族

奧賽羅：貴族摩爾人，威尼斯軍事將領

凱西奧：奧賽羅的忠誠副將

以阿哥：奧賽羅的旗官，惡徒

羅德里戈：容易受騙的年輕紳士

蒙塔諾：在奧賽羅之前的賽浦勒斯總督

小丑：奧賽羅的僕人

黛絲德夢娜：柏拉班修的女兒，奧賽羅年輕又美麗的新娘

艾米莉亞：以阿哥的妻子

畢昂嘉：一名妓女

紳士們、**水手們**、**軍官們**、**信差**、**傳令官**、**樂師們**、**僕人們**，以及**元老們**（**先生們**）

第一幕

第一場

P. 007

（羅德里戈與以阿哥上，在威尼斯的一條街道。）

羅德里戈：你為何沒早點告訴我？

以阿哥：你橫豎也不會聽我說。

羅德里戈：但是你曾說過你憎恨他——

以阿哥：是的，我本應成為他的副將，而他卻提拔了麥可凱西奧。凱西奧未曾上過戰場證明自己的實力；至於我，我多次領兵征戰，卻僅只是奧賽羅的旗官，最低階層的軍官！

羅德里戈：我寧可當他的絞刑吏。

以阿哥：對於現行的新體制，重要的是你認識的人脈——而非你有何實力。先生，請你自行判斷我是否有理由忠愛那個摩爾人。

羅德里戈：那你為何跟隨他？

以阿哥：莫要被蒙騙了，我跟隨他只是為了報復他。我們不可能人人居於統領之位——而居於統領之位者亦不可能被所有人忠心跟隨。我跟隨他是為了自身的利益；但求上天為證，我的言行舉止皆非出於愛和責任，即便我必須表現出效力於他。我其實不似表象那般。

羅德里戈：我們不能容許他為所欲為！

以阿哥：讓我們去喚醒黛絲德夢娜的父親，他的憤怒將會削減奧賽羅的喜悅。

羅德里戈：此即她父親的住處。

以阿哥：喊醒他！彷彿城鎮著火似地大喊！

羅德里戈：你好！柏拉班修！柏拉班修先生！你好！

以阿哥：醒一醒，柏拉班修！有小偷！有小偷！

柏拉班修（從樓上的一扇窗戶探頭）：為何如此大呼小叫？發生何事？

羅德里戈：天啊，先生，有人盜取你的財物！你心暴怒，靈魂喪失了一半。就在此刻，有隻公黑羊正在與你的母白羊交媾。起來！敲響鐘聲喚醒你的鄰居們，否則那魔鬼將使你成為一名祖父。

柏拉班修：你喪失心智了嗎？你是何人？

羅德里戈：我是羅德里戈，先生，你認不得我的聲音嗎？

柏拉班修：此地不歡迎你！我早已言明不會將女兒許配予你。

羅德里戈：我前來拜託是為了再單純再不過的原因。

以阿哥（附和羅德里戈）：我們是來幫助你的。倘若你再不快點行動，令嬡就要和一匹摩爾馬交媾了，你即將擁有一群戰馬似的孫子們。

柏拉班修：你說這是什麼鬼話？

以阿哥：此乃實情，先生，令嬡正和那摩爾人像兩頭野獸一般在交媾。

柏拉班修：惡徒！你要為此言付出代價。

羅德里戈：先生，我願付出任何代價。或許你意欲你美麗的女兒在大半夜裡，投入好色摩爾人的粗鄙懷抱中；倘若如此，我們便很抱歉打擾了你，但是你若事先並不知情，那你就應該感謝我們。不如你親自前往一探究竟？倘若她在她的閨房或你的府上，便是我欺騙你，我願任憑你依法處置。

柏拉班修：給我蠟燭！喚醒府內所有的人！我說給我燭火！燭火！

（他從樓上的陽台下。）

以阿哥（對羅德里戈）**：**再見了，我必須先行一步，作為對奧賽羅不利之事的目擊者對我並無助益。我已知他深得國家之器重。喔，他或許會得到輕微的懲處，但是國家需要他領軍與賽浦勒斯作戰。縱使我憎恨他，但我還是必須明顯表示對他的忠愛。帶人前往客棧搜查，我會和他在那兒等你。再見了！

（以阿哥下，柏拉班修從底下上，僕人們帶著火炬隨他而來。）

柏拉班修：此事著實邪惡不堪，她果真不在！我這遲暮殘生將只剩下悲苦。說吧，羅德里戈，你在何處見著她？喔，那個傻丫頭！你說她正和那摩爾人一起嗎？喔，背叛血統啊！你怎能確知那就是她？喔，她欺騙了我！叫醒我的家人！你認為他們已有婚約嗎？

羅德里戈：是的，我確實這麼認為。

柏拉班修：喔，天啊！她是如何外出的？竟如此欺騙我！從今爾後，父親們莫因女兒們的行徑，就誤信她們的心意。難道是妖法所致，使得年輕貞潔的少女遭到玷汙？羅德里戈，你是否讀過書上有類似的記載？

羅德里戈：是的，先生，我確實讀過。

柏拉班修：喔，早知道我就將她許配給你！你知道我們在何處能尋得她和那摩爾人？

羅德里戈：我想我能找到他們。

柏拉班修：請帶路！好羅德里戈，事成之後我必有重賞。

第二場

P. 013

（奧賽羅、以阿哥與僕人們上，在另一條街道。）

以阿哥：雖然我在戰場上殺過人，但殺人仍是有違我的良心；我的惡念不夠滿足我自身的需求。我曾有過九次或十次想要刺殺柏拉班修的這裡，在肋骨下方。

奧賽羅：此乃不智之舉。

以阿哥：但是他出言不遜，無禮地羞辱你，我情不自禁地想懲治他！但是請問你，先生——你們是否完成婚禮？此事你可以確定：柏拉班修將拆散你們的婚姻，或是依法對你提出莫名其妙的控訴。

奧賽羅：隨他去施盡卑劣手段吧，我效力於國家的貢獻，將不會因他們的抱怨所消弭。此事尚且無人知曉，但是等待時機成熟，我將公諸於世我乃皇室成員之後裔的事實；我能要求取得和內人同等的財富。你要知道，以阿哥：倘若我不是深愛著溫柔的黛絲德夢娜，縱然給我海裡的所有財寶，我也不會放棄我的自由。但是你瞧！朝我們而來的是什麼火光？

（凱西奧與其他軍官們上，後面跟隨手持火炬的僕人們。）

以阿哥：那是被喚醒的父親和他的朋友們！你還是進屋躲躲吧。

奧賽羅：不，我必須被他們找到。我的才能、我的頭銜和我完美的靈魂，都將為我的見證，不是嗎？

以阿哥：我倒是不以為然。

奧賽羅（對凱西奧一行人）：你好，朋友們！有何消息？

凱西奧：公爵差我來問候你，將軍，他要即刻面見你。

奧賽羅：你認為他所為何事？

凱西奧：應該是來自賽浦勒斯的消息，已有許多重要人士前去與公爵會合，他們也在召喚你前去。當他們在你府上未能尋得你之時，元老院派了三組人馬四處找你。

奧賽羅：所幸你們找到我了。我先去知會家人我要出門，然後我就隨你們同往。

（他下。）

凱西奧（對以阿哥）：旗官，奧賽羅何以在此？

以阿哥：老實告訴你，他今晚登上了一艘富裕的船。倘若那是合法的獎賞，那他就有一生享用不盡的財富了。

凱西奧：我不明白。

以阿哥：他已成婚。

凱西奧：對方是何人？

（奧賽羅再上。）

以阿哥：哎呀，就是——來吧，將軍，準備出發了嗎？

奧賽羅：我準備好了。

凱西奧：又有一組人馬前來找你。

（柏拉班修、羅德里戈與軍官們手持火炬與武器上。）

以阿哥：是柏拉班修！將軍，務必提防：他是懷著惡意前來。

奧賽羅：你好！但請留步！

羅德里戈（對柏拉班修）：先生，是那摩爾人。

柏拉班修：抓住他，那個竊賊！

（兩群人拔劍相對。）

奧賽羅：收起你們的利劍，沾了露水會生鏽的。（**對柏拉班修：**）老先生，有話好說，你這般年紀用智慧總好過動武。

柏拉班修：喔，你這可惡的竊賊！你將小女藏於何處？你對她施了妖法，否則像她那樣的女孩——如此溫柔、美麗又快活——何以會與你交好？她拒絕了威尼斯最好的男人們，想必是你以咒語蠱惑她！你必定是施以藥物或丹方，削弱了她的意志，所以我要逮捕你，控告你施行禁術之罪。

奧賽羅：我要前去何處回應你的這番指控？

柏拉班修：前去監牢，直到法庭傳喚你去接受審判。

奧賽羅：我很樂意服從，但是公爵派了這些信差們（**指著凱西奧一行人**）要帶我前去面見他，我該如何向他交代？

柏拉班修：什麼？公爵到這深夜還在議事？我們去見他！我此事非同小可，公爵也會認同此事邪惡，將易地而處來決斷此事。倘若你做了此等行徑卻還能自由離去，那奴隸和異教徒們將在我國從政。

第三場

P. 018

（公爵與元老們坐在議事室的桌旁。）

公爵（指著桌上的幾封信件）：這些報告可謂是眾說紛紜。

元老一：是啊，他們的說法各異，我的是說一百零七艘船隻。

公爵：我的報告是說一百四十艘。

元老二：我的是說兩百艘！他們對數字的記錄莫衷一是——但是他們都認同有支土耳其艦隊正朝向賽浦勒斯接近。

公爵：是啊，這消息似乎甚是明確。

元老一：柏拉班修和那英勇的摩爾人來了。

（柏拉班修、奧賽羅、凱西奧、以阿哥、羅德里戈與軍官們上。）

公爵：英勇的奧賽羅，我們必須派你去對抗敵軍土耳其人。（對柏拉班修：）喔！我方才沒看到你。歡迎你，尊貴的先生，今晚少了你的忠言和協助。

柏拉班修：我亦是深感遺憾。好閣下，請寬恕我，令我從床上起身的並非我的職責，或聽聞你要議事。將我從睡夢中驚醒者亦非國家大事。我此刻內心甚是悲傷，掩蓋和吞沒了其餘所有的憂愁。

公爵：為什麼？所為何事？

柏拉班修：我的女兒！喔，我的女兒！

元老一：死了？

柏拉班修：是的，於我而言！她受人欺騙，從我身邊被拐走了，有人從江湖術士那兒買來邪藥，下蠱使她墮落敗德。以她的本性是不可能有此行為——所以她必定是受到巫術所使。

公爵：我誓言凡有此犯行之人，必定嚴懲不貸——即便是我的親生兒子也難倖免。

柏拉班修：我謙恭地感謝閣下。罪人在此——正是這摩爾人——你派遣信差們召喚而來的這個人。

公爵（對奧賽羅）：你為此作何辯解？

奧賽羅：最高尚和尊貴的先生們，我確實帶走了這位老先生的女兒。是的，我已經娶她為妻，我的滔天罪行莫過於此。我並非天生舌燦蓮花之人，但是倘若給我發言的機會，我將忠實地敘述我的愛情故事，與我用來贏取她女兒芳心的愛情魔法（因這乃是我被指控的罪名）。

柏拉班修：這丫頭向來不是大膽之人，她的天性恬靜，略動感情就會滿臉羞紅，因此我要再次言明，他必定是對她下了強效藥。

公爵：你此番誓言無法證明什麼；缺乏證據，你也不能任意誹謗他。

奧賽羅：請閣下差人將小姐找來，讓她當著她父親的面述說她對我的印象。倘若她道了我的不是，儘管剝奪你已賜予我的榮譽，然後判我死刑。

公爵：帶黛絲德夢娜來此。

（兩、三個人下。）

奧賽羅（對以阿哥）：旗官，你帶路吧，你知道她在何處。（以阿哥下。）（對公爵與元老們：）在她來此之前，我要告訴你們我和這位美麗的姑娘是如何墜入愛河的。她父親對我很是器重，經常邀我至他府上作客。他要我敘述我的生平事蹟，我講述了幾次危險的旅行，以及在洪水期間和戰場上的可怕意外；還說了我被敵軍俘虜、販賣為奴之事；也提到我逃走之後在巨大洞穴和荒涼沙漠中的冒險。黛絲德夢娜聽得出神，直到她有家事要做而不得不離席。她只要逮到機會，就會再回座聽我陳述，用貪婪的耳朵吞噬我的故事。某日，我在閒暇之餘，將我的故事一口氣對她說完；在此之前，她只零零星星地聽了片段。當我提及我年少之時的不幸，她經常掩面哭泣。待我說完我這不可思議又悲傷的故事之後，她說她祈求上天能賜給她如是的伴侶，還說我若是有朋友心儀她，便要我教他如何敘述我的故事，如此追求她便可。我明白她的暗示，也向她表白我的心意。她愛我是因我曾經歷過的危險，我愛她是因她被我的故事深深感動；此即我唯一施予她的妖術。那位小姐來了，讓她自己說個清楚吧。

（黛絲德夢娜、以阿哥與侍從們上。）

公爵（竊語）：換作是我的女兒，此般的故事亦能打動她！好柏拉班修，你得善加利用才是。

柏拉班修：我懇求你，讓她說吧。倘若她說是她主動暗示他來追求，那就因著我對奧賽羅不公正的指責而懲罰我！（對黛絲德夢娜：）過來，好姑娘，在座何人是你最應該順服的？

黛絲德夢娜：我此刻兼負雙重責任，我尊貴的父親。我承蒙你的生育和教養之恩，因我是你的女兒，但這位是我的夫君，如同我母親對你克盡人妻之責、將你置於比她父親更重要的地位，我對這摩爾人也必須比照對待，他是我的夫君。

柏拉班修（對黛絲德夢娜）：願上帝與你同在！我已無話可說。

公爵（對柏拉班修）：讓我說句話幫助你接受這對愛侶。哀悼過去的不幸，必然會招致更多不幸；聰明之人遭竊毫不在意，痛苦流涕反而傷害自己。現在我們必須商議國事了，土耳其人正大舉進犯賽浦勒斯。奧賽羅，你是前去抵禦敵軍的最佳人選。

奧賽羅：我會去的，但是我的妻子需要有個安置她的家。

公爵：倘若你願意的話，就讓她與她父親同住吧。

柏拉班修：如此我恕難從命！

奧賽羅：我亦如此。

黛絲德夢娜：我亦然，讓我隨奧賽羅去吧。

奧賽羅：請閣下恩准她與我同往。倘若她在我身邊時我怠忽職守，就讓持家的主婦們用我的頭盔做成平底鍋，讓邪惡攻擊我的好名聲！

公爵：她的去留由你決定。賽浦勒斯的情勢告急；奧賽羅，你必須在一小時之後啟程。（**對柏拉班修：**）高貴的先生，倘若才德是美麗的表徵，令婿可謂是比黑色要美麗得多啊！

柏拉班修（**對奧賽羅**）**：**你要看好她，摩爾人，她已欺騙了父親，也有可能欺騙你。

（**柏拉班修、公爵、元老們與軍官們下。**）

奧賽羅：我願用生命擔保她的忠貞！誠實的以阿哥，我必須將黛絲德夢娜交付予你照顧，直到她準備好隨我同赴戰場，請尊夫人悉心關照她，待時機成熟之時再護送她倆啟程。來吧，黛絲德夢娜，我們只剩下一小時，必須恪遵時程。

（**奧賽羅與黛絲德夢娜下。**）

羅德里戈：以阿哥，我該如何是好？

以阿哥：哎呀，就上床睡覺吧。

羅德里戈：我恨不得去投水自盡。

以阿哥：你真是太傻了！

羅德里戈：在生不如死之際，活著才是愚蠢之舉。

以阿哥：來吧，像個男人！投水自盡？該溺死的是貓和瞎眼的小狗！我是以你朋友的身分相勸，將錢放入你的錢袋中，上戰場吧。過不了多久，黛絲德夢娜就會厭煩了那摩爾人；奧賽羅之於她是老牛吃嫩草，她會再另找年輕的小伙子，所以你要竭盡所能地掙錢，她未幾將成為你的囊中物，別再想著投水自盡了，寧可冒險為了滿足自己的欲望而被絞死。說什麼自盡，真是該死！

羅德里戈：你此言可有憑據？

以阿哥：你大可相信我。去吧，多掙點錢！我已重複多遍，現在就再告訴你一次——我憎恨那摩爾人，打從心底恨透他；你也有充分的理由憎恨他，就讓我們互助合作，聯手報復他吧。此事留待明日再到我的住處詳談。

羅德里戈：我會提早到達。

以阿哥：去吧，晚安，別再說什麼投水自盡了，聽見沒？

羅德里戈：我已改頭換面，這就去變賣我所有的土地。

（羅德里戈下。）

以阿哥：我就是這樣利用傻瓜去掙錢使我得利！我有充分的理由憎恨那摩爾人，流言謠傳他勾引我的妻子，細微的徵兆足夠使我相信此事。奧賽羅對我頗為信任，如此能使我更容易復仇。凱西奧是個彬彬有禮的俊美男子，讓我來想想辦法——我該如何利用此一優勢？有了，我來向奧賽羅進言，說凱西奧和她的妻子過從甚密；如凱西奧這般長相俊美的男人，天生就會使女人變節不忠。那摩爾人的天性自由開放，他看見人家裝出一副忠厚老實的模樣，就以為他是好人，是的，我將能輕易地欺騙他。我想到了！就這麼決定！地獄和黑夜必然會揭露此邪惡計畫。

（下。）

第二幕

第一場 P. 031

（蒙塔諾與兩名紳士上，在暴風雨肆虐中來到賽浦勒斯的一處海港。）

蒙塔諾：我未曾見過如此狂烈的暴風雨，你認為情勢會如何發展？

紳士二：土耳其艦隊必定會被摧毀，絕對不可能倖免於難。

（紳士三上。）

紳士三：有消息，各位！戰爭已然結束！這片惡水摧毀了土耳其船艦，一艘威尼斯皇家船艦目擊了可怕的船骸，以及多數土耳其艦隊所蒙受的苦難。那艘船已在此登陸，有個來自維洛那的人上了岸，他名喚麥可凱西奧，那個好戰摩爾人的副將。那摩爾人自己仍在海上，正朝此地過來。

蒙塔諾：聽聞此事我滿心歡喜，奧賽羅將是統治此地的不二人選。

紳士三：但是凱西奧雖然回報了土耳其傷亡損失的好消息，仍非常擔憂那摩爾人的安危。

蒙塔諾：讓我們祈禱他平安無事。

（凱西奧上。）

凱西奧：謝謝你們，這個飽受戰火摧殘的島上英勇的人們，你們都崇敬那摩爾人！喔，讓上天保佑他平安！

蒙塔諾：他是否有艘好船艦？

凱西奧：他的船艦很堅固，領航員的技術過人。

（從舞台後方傳來一個聲音：「有帆船、有帆船、有帆船！」）

凱西奧（對紳士二）：先生，去看看來者何人。

紳士二：我這就去。（他下。）

蒙塔諾：好副將，你的將領是否已婚？

凱西奧：是的，他的妻子相貌美麗又有無瑕的名聲。

（紳士二再上。）

紳士二：將軍的旗官以阿哥已然登陸。

凱西奧：如此甚好，他帶著美麗的黛絲德夢娜隨行。

蒙塔諾：她是何人？

凱西奧：奧賽羅的好妻子，她被交由以阿哥保護。但願上天保佑奧賽羅，平安來到黛絲德夢娜的懷中。（黛絲德夢娜、艾米莉亞、以阿哥、羅德里戈與侍從們上。）你好，夫人！願上天之恩賜將你圍繞。

黛絲德夢娜：謝謝你，凱西奧。你有否我夫君的消息？

凱西奧：我只知他平安無恙，未幾即會抵達此地。

黛絲德夢娜：喔，但是我心憂懼！你們的船艦是如何失散？

凱西奧：是暴風雨將我們分散，但是你聽！

（從舞台後方傳來一個聲音喊著：「有帆船、有帆船！」）

凱西奧：去看看來者何人。（紳士二下。）（對以阿哥：）好旗官，歡迎你。（對艾米莉亞：）歡迎你，夫人。（凱西奧親吻艾米莉亞的手，接著他也親吻黛絲德夢娜的手。）（對以阿哥：）希望你不介意才好，好以阿哥。我如此大膽地表示禮貌，乃我自小接受之教養薰陶使然。

以阿哥（自言自語）：好啊！他親吻她的手。佈下這個小小的網，我即可捕獲凱西奧這般的大蒼蠅。好，對著她微笑——笑吧！我會用你自身的禮貌將你一軍。倘若你的行徑使你失去了軍職，你會後悔當了這麼一個謙恭有禮的紳士！非常好，這一吻來得好！這禮貌甚是周到！（從舞台後方傳來號角聲。）（對凱西奧：）是那摩爾人！我認得他的號角聲。

（奧賽羅與侍從們上。）

奧賽羅：喔，我靈魂的喜悅！

黛絲德夢娜：我親愛的奧賽羅！

（奧賽羅親吻黛絲德夢娜。）

以阿哥（竊語）：喔，你們此刻是琴瑟和鳴！但是我會摧毀這奏出和諧樂音的琴弦，我言出必行。

奧賽羅：來吧，我們前去城堡。有消息，朋友們！我們的戰爭已然結束，土耳其人都溺死了。（對黛絲德夢娜：）你在賽浦勒斯必受寵愛，親愛的——我已在此地感受到熱情。

（除了以阿哥與羅德里戈之外，眾人下。）

以阿哥（對羅德里戈）：稍後在港口與我會合，不見不散。凱西奧今晚會在衛兵哨亭站哨，但首先我必須告訴你：黛絲德夢娜對他愛得如癡如狂。

羅德里戈：愛上凱西奧？哎呀，這是不可能的事！

以阿哥：安靜點，仔細聽我道來。猶記她最初如何癡愛那摩爾人嗎？只因他吹噓自己、對她說些天花亂墜的謊言？她會只為了聽他聒絮不休而繼續愛他嗎？你莫要相信此等謬事，她需要的是與她年齡較為相仿的男人，於是天性驅使她另覓新歡；而凱西奧是顯而易見的選擇，他是個口蜜腹劍的惡徒，況且他還長相俊美！他擁有所有年輕的傻丫頭們所渴求的一切特質，是個不折不扣的敗德之徒。那女人早已愛上他！

羅德里戈：我無法相信她會如此水性楊花，她擁有聖潔的本性。

以阿哥：什麼聖潔全是瞎說！倘若她是真的聖潔，她就不可能愛上那摩爾人。什麼聖潔全是胡謅！你沒看到凱西奧親吻她的手嗎？

羅德里戈：是的，我看到了，那只是禮貌性的親吻。

以阿哥：那是淫亂之舉，我告訴你！他們的嘴唇如此貼近，他們的氣息早已相互擁抱！哼！但是先生，請照我的話去做，今晚仔細觀察，凱西奧並不認識你，想個辦法激怒他，說話太大聲，或是辱罵冒犯他——你當下想到什麼就怎麼做，他的脾氣暴躁易怒，或許他會試圖毆打你，你要竭盡所能挑釁他至此般境地，如此我便能讓凱西奧解職，將他逐出賽浦勒斯；如此一來，你即可更快地接近黛絲德夢娜。但是首先，我們必須除去橫在你我面前的一道阻礙。

羅德里戈：我會照辦，只要此舉能使我占得優勢。

以阿哥：我保證一定會的！稍後在城堡與我會合，再見。

羅德里戈：再見。

（羅德里戈下。）

以阿哥（竊語）**：**我確實認定凱西奧是愛她的，她自然也有可能愛上他。縱使我憎恨他，但是那摩爾人擁有忠實、專情又崇高的本性，我相信他會對她恪守為人夫之責。現在，我也愛她——但是並非出於情慾；我愛她是因為她會幫我報復，因我懷疑那好色的摩爾人勾引了我的妻子，我想到就忿恨難消。除非我對奧賽羅以牙還牙、一妻抵一妻，否則我決不善罷甘休。即便我無法徹底達到目的，我仍會使他嫉妒到理智難以平復之境地。為達此目標，那個無用的威尼斯人羅德里戈必須照我的話去做，麥可凱西奧便能成為我的囊中物（因我恐怕凱西奧也早已爬上我妻子的枕畔）。我如此地徹底愚弄他，那摩爾人可要感謝我、愛我和獎賞我了！此乃我的計畫，雖然仍有點紊亂無條理；要等到為時已晚之時，才能看清邪惡的臉孔。

●第二場

P. 040

（一名傳令官上，帶著一份公告書走上街頭。）

傳令官：奧賽羅希望大家慶祝土耳其艦隊全軍覆沒；跳舞的跳舞，生營火的生營火，但是每個人都要盡興狂歡，因為這也是他的婚禮慶典！開放所有的廚房，從此刻五點鐘開始到鐘聲敲響十一點為止，皆提供免費的餐食茶點。願上天保佑賽浦勒斯島，以及我們尊貴的奧賽羅將軍！

（全體下。）

●第三場

P. 041

（在城堡；奧賽羅、黛絲德夢娜、凱西奧與侍從們上。）

奧賽羅：好凱西奧，你今晚負責守夜，務必確保慶祝活動不會失控。暫且向你道聲晚安。（對黛絲德夢娜：）來吧，我親愛的妻子。

（奧賽羅、黛絲德夢娜與侍從們下；以阿哥上。）

凱西奧：歡迎你，以阿哥。我們現在必須去守夜了。

以阿哥：且慢，副將，此刻尚未十點鐘！我這兒有點酒，讓我們共飲之，同為奧賽羅那黑將軍乾一杯。

凱西奧：我已經喝多了，不能再多飲黃湯。

以阿哥：什麼？這是縱情狂歡的夜晚，有些朋友在等著與我們同歡。去吧，喚他們過來。

凱西奧：我這就去辦——但是我認為此舉不妥。

（凱西奧下。）

以阿哥（竊語）：他今晚已經喝得夠多了，務必再灌他一杯酒，如此他便能更容易與人爭執和衝突。那個犯相思病的傻子羅德里戈，今晚一直在向黛絲德夢娜敬酒，明知道他要輪值守夜，還杯杯飲盡見底。目前正在守夜的三個賽浦勒斯小夥子，我也一杯接一杯地灌醉了他們。如今有這麼多人爛醉如泥，我這就來挑釁凱西奧做出使全島大亂之行徑。他們來了！

（凱西奧、蒙塔諾與紳士們上，僕人們帶著酒尾隨在後。）

凱西奧：天啊，我已經喝了一大杯酒。

蒙塔諾：快來吧！再飲一小杯無妨，才不過小小一杯。

以阿哥：這兒要斟點酒！

（以阿哥唱了幾首飲酒歌，凱西奧頗為讚賞。男人們繼續喝酒，舉杯同祝奧賽羅健康。最後，凱西奧準備要離開。）

凱西奧：我們該去辦點正事了。莫要以為我酒醉了，各位。（指著以阿哥：）這是我的旗官。（舉起雙手：）這是我的右手，這是我的左手。我並未喝醉，還能站著好好說話。

（凱西奧下，顯然是喝醉了。）

蒙塔諾：來吧，各位，我們該去守夜了。

以阿哥（指著凱西奧的方向）：你看到他了嗎？凱西奧是配得上站在凱撒身旁發號施令之人，但是你看看他的此等罪行，和他的德行完全等同——德行有多好、罪行就有多重。由於凱西奧的弱點，我恐怕奧賽羅對他如此信任，有朝一日會在這座島上招致禍亂。

蒙塔諾：但是他經常如此嗎？

以阿哥：向來如此，在他就寢之前。倘若他沒有因酒醉入睡，他便會徹夜不眠。

蒙塔諾：將軍是否知情？此事還是知會他為宜。

（羅德里戈上。）

以阿哥（對羅德里戈竊語）**：**你來此所為何事，羅德里戈？快隨副將去！

（羅德里戈下。）

蒙塔諾：很遺憾那尊貴的摩爾人，竟安排如此重要的職務給一個能力不足之人。還是向那摩爾人說個清楚才是明智之舉。

以阿哥：即使用這整座美麗的島嶼交換，我也不會這麼做！我非常敬愛凱西奧，我會試圖協助他解決他的問題。但是你聽！那是什麼聲音？

（從舞台後方傳來一個聲音喊著「救命！」。凱西奧上，對羅德里戈窮追不捨。）

凱西奧：可恨，你這惡徒！你這無賴！

蒙塔諾：怎麼回事，副將？

凱西奧：我難道需要一個惡徒來教我如何盡責行事？我要打到這惡棍知道長幼尊卑為止！

羅德里戈：打我？

凱西奧：還在喋喋不休？（他毆打羅德里戈。）

蒙塔諾：不，凱西奧！（他抓住凱西奧的手臂。）莫要再打了。

凱西奧：放開我，先生，否則我一拳打破你的頭。

蒙塔諾：好了啦，你喝醉了！

凱西奧：喝醉？（**蒙塔諾與凱西奧打鬥。**）

以阿哥（**向羅德里戈竊語**）**：**你快走！去警告眾人有叛變情事。（**羅德里戈下。**）停止打鬥，好副將。真是夠了，各位！

（**從舞台後方傳來鐘聲，喚醒整個城鎮。奧賽羅與侍從們上。**）

奧賽羅：這是怎麼回事？此次爭端是如何引起的？難道我們成了土耳其人？我們要對自己人做上天阻止土耳其人做的事嗎？說話啊，是何人起頭？

以阿哥：我不知道，他們方才還稱兄道弟，突然就拔劍相向開始冷血打鬥了。我無法回答你是何人起頭。

奧賽羅：凱西奧，你如何捲入其中？

凱西奧：請原諒我，我無法言語。

奧賽羅：蒙塔諾，發生了什麼事？

蒙塔諾：尊貴的奧賽羅，我身負重傷，方才只是出於自衛而反擊。

奧賽羅：現在我想知道此次爭端如何起始、是何人起的頭。證明有罪之人——即便是我的孿生兄弟——也會失去我的友誼。此事實在過分！以阿哥，究竟是何人起頭？

以阿哥：我寧可割掉舌頭，也不願說出對麥可凱西奧不利之言語，然而我相信說出真相應該不會傷害他。那我就說了，將軍。方才我和蒙塔諾在此處談話，突然有個人跑來呼救，凱西奧手持著劍尾隨在後，意圖殺了他。先生，在我和蒙塔諾試圖阻止凱西奧之時，另一個人跑走了，我想追上去，但是他跑得比我快。我迅速回到此處，因我聽到劍擊聲，以及凱西奧在大聲咒罵。直到今晚之前，我絕不會對他有如此之評論，但是人非聖賢、孰能無過——即使是最優秀的人偶爾也會犯錯，我相信凱西奧必定是受到跑走之人的某種羞辱，他是忍無可忍才會出手。

奧賽羅：以阿哥，你是因為誠實和友愛才會寬恕凱西奧。凱西奧，我友愛你——但你將不再是我麾下的軍官了。

（黛絲德夢娜上，帶著侍從們。）

黛絲德夢娜：怎麼回事，親愛的？

奧賽羅：現在沒事了，甜心，你快去睡吧。（對蒙塔諾：）先生，我的醫生會為你療傷。（對侍從們：）帶他去吧。（蒙塔諾下，帶著侍從們。）以阿哥，安撫受此爭端驚擾之人。來吧，黛絲德夢娜，平靜的睡眠被爭鬥所驚擾是軍旅生涯常有之事。

（全體下，獨留以阿哥與凱西奧。）

以阿哥：你有受傷嗎，副將？

凱西奧：有，已是傷重難以醫治了。

以阿哥：喔，不會吧！

凱西奧：名譽、名譽、名譽！喔，我已喪失了我的名譽！

以阿哥：名譽乃愚蠢之事，經常是得之無益、失之無損。來吧，弟兄！你未幾即可重獲將軍之寵信。向他求情吧——他會聽的。

凱西奧：我寧可懇求他憎恨我，也不願求他原諒如此卑劣的醉酒軍官。酒醉？喋喋不休？打鬥？咒罵？喔，酒這無形的靈啊，讓我們喚你為惡魔！

以阿哥：方才與你打鬥的是何人？他對你做了何事？

凱西奧：我不知道，來龍去脈我都記不清了。

以阿哥：哎呀，你現在倒是看似清醒，何以恢復得如此之快？

凱西奧：醉酒的惡魔屈服於憤怒的惡魔了，一個瑕疵引我走向另一個。喔，我好恨我自己！

以阿哥：莫要如此苛責自己。但願這一切都沒發生過，然而米已成粥，就好好替自己謀劃吧。

凱西奧：倘若我再求他還我職銜，他會指控我是個醉鬼！

以阿哥：我來告訴你該怎麼做。將軍的夫人對他的影響甚鉅，去請她幫忙，她愛好自由、慈悲為懷、心地善良。她認為他人對她有所要求，不多做一點就是錯的；我用我全部的財產打賭她必定會幫你！

凱西奧：你的建議甚好。

以阿哥：我向你保證，此言乃出於我對你真摯的敬愛和誠實的良善。

凱西奧：我相信你。待天亮之後，我會去懇求黛絲德夢娜的幫忙。

以阿哥：你這麼做就對了，晚安吧。

凱西奧：晚安，誠實的以阿哥。

（**凱西奧下。**）

以阿哥（竊語）**：**我提供如此的好建議，有誰會說我是個惡徒？贏得黛絲德夢娜的支持，是凱西奧唯一的希望，但是在她向那摩爾人求情之時，我會將毒藥倒入他的耳朵，我會說她乃因與凱西奧有姦情而前來懇求。她愈是試圖幫他，看在那摩爾人的眼裡就會更加疑心。如此一來，我便將她的美德化作邪惡；我會利用她的善良，編織一張網捕獲他們所有的人！（羅德里戈上。）怎麼了，羅德里戈？

羅德里戈：我今晚挨了一頓好打，疼痛難耐卻只換來一頓教訓。我的錢財幾乎耗盡，所以我未幾即須返回威尼斯。

以阿哥：缺乏耐性之人真是可悲！有什麼傷口不是慢慢癒合的？凱西奧或許打了你，但是你毀了凱西奧。要有耐心，快去睡吧，你很快就會明白的。快去！（羅德里戈下。）有兩件事必須去做：我去向那摩爾人進獻讒言，同時讓我的妻子去找黛絲德夢娜訴說凱西奧之事。正當凱西奧在向黛絲德夢娜求情之時，我就帶著奧賽羅過來。對，就這麼辦！我不能再遲疑，免得壞了這個妙計。

（以阿哥下。）

第三幕

●第一場

P. 055

（凱西奧與以阿哥上，在賽浦勒斯的城堡前面。）

凱西奧：以阿哥，能否請尊夫人安排與黛絲德夢娜見面？

以阿哥：我這就去找艾米莉亞，然後設法分散那摩爾人的注意力。

凱西奧：我謙恭地感謝你。（**以阿哥下。**）你是個善良又誠實的人。

（艾米莉亞上。）

艾米莉亞：日安，好副將，你所遭遇的事令我感到遺憾，但是一切未幾即會好轉，黛絲德夢娜一直在為你說情。

凱西奧：但是我仍要懇求你，給我機會單獨與她相談。

艾米莉亞：那就請進吧，先生，我這就帶你去找她。

凱西奧：為此我對你銘感五內。

（艾米莉亞與凱西奧下。）

●第二場

P. 056

（黛絲德夢娜、凱西奧與艾米莉亞上，在城堡的花園中。）

黛絲德夢娜：請你放心，好凱西奧，我必會竭力幫你。

凱西奧：親愛的夫人，我將永遠是你忠實的僕人。

黛絲德夢娜：我知道，也感謝你，此事包在我身上。倘若我因友誼而有所承諾，我必定會全力以赴。我的夫君從不休息，我會耗盡他的耐心，無論他做何事我都會提到你的職務，所以請你放寬心，我寧死也不辜負你所託。

（奧賽羅與以阿哥上。）

凱西奧：夫人，我先行告退。

黛絲德夢娜：哎呀，留下來聽我把話說。

凱西奧：現在不方便，夫人，此般場面令我不太自在。

黛絲德夢娜：那就隨你的意吧。

（凱西奧下。）

以阿哥：哎呀！我不喜歡那樣。

奧賽羅：你說什麼？

以阿哥：沒什麼，閣下。

奧賽羅：方才與內人談話者不是凱西奧嗎？

以阿哥：凱西奧，閣下？不是，否則他見你過來就不會心虛地溜走了。

奧賽羅：我認為那就是他。

黛絲德夢娜：你好，夫君！我方才在和凱西奧談話。倘若我有能力影響你的決定，這次請接受他的道歉吧，他是真的敬重你！若非如此，就是我識人不清了。請你將他的職務交還予他。

奧賽羅：現在不行，親愛的黛絲德夢娜，此事我們改日再談。

黛絲德夢娜：求求你，親愛的，告訴我何時才能談！切莫超過三天，他是真心悔過。你也知道的，倘若你對我有所要求，我也會應允你的所求。你何以拒絕我簡單的請求？

奧賽羅：請你莫再多說，他若有所求大可直接來找我。我是不會拒絕你的！現在我要你這樣做：請你暫且稍作回避。

黛絲德夢娜：要我拒絕你嗎？不！再見了，夫君。

（黛絲德夢娜與艾米莉亞下。）

奧賽羅：果真是可恥之人！惡魔取走了我的靈魂，但我是真的愛你！

以阿哥：我尊貴的閣下——

奧賽羅：怎麼了，以阿哥？

以阿哥：當你向夫人求婚之時，凱西奧就知道你對她的愛嗎？

奧賽羅：是的，自始至終他都知情。你為何這麼問？

以阿哥：喔，我只是好奇一問。

奧賽羅：好奇什麼，以阿哥？

以阿哥：我不知他與夫人早已相識。

奧賽羅：喔，是的，他經常為我倆傳話。

以阿哥：是嗎？

奧賽羅：是啊！你認為有所不妥嗎？請將你的想法告知予我，說出你最壞的想法。

以阿哥：你是要我說出我的想法嗎，好閣下？萬一是無禮的不實指控呢？有哪個心地純潔之人不會偶爾掠過污穢的想法？

奧賽羅：倘若你認為你的朋友遭人欺侮，又未將你的想法告知予他，以阿哥，那你就是在傷害他了。

以阿哥：既然我可能被誤解，那我寧可不說出內心的想法。

奧賽羅：你此話是何意？

以阿哥：不論男女的好名聲，親愛的閣下，是靈魂最重要的寶石。偷走我錢袋之人得到的是垃圾，它原本是很重要，但如今成了身外之物；它曾是我的，如今成了他的，而它也曾屬於數以千計的其他人。但是取走我的好名聲之人，他奪走之物無法使他富有，卻使我變得貧窮。

奧賽羅：天啊，我命令你將你的想法告訴我！

以阿哥：閣下，要留心嫉妒啊！那是嘲笑獵物的綠眼妖魔。男人確定妻子不忠，比疑心妻子出軌來的好。男人在愛慕的同時亦心生疑慮，深愛著對方，卻又滿腹狐疑，那簡直是度日如年！

奧賽羅：你何以這麼說？你說我的妻子貌美、錦衣玉食、喜好有人陪伴、言論自由、歌舞技藝過人，是無法使我心生嫉妒的。就品德高尚之人而言，這些不過是美德罷了。雖然我並不完美，但是我不會懷疑她的愛。她慧眼獨具，所以選中我。不，以阿哥，我必須親眼見到證據才會心起疑惑；而當我疑惑之時，我必須先行證實。倘若證據確鑿，我會快刀斬亂麻，不會再有愛或嫉妒！

以阿哥：聽你這麼說我很高興。我未能舉證，但是請留意尊夫人的言行！當她和凱西奧相處之時，請仔細觀察她。莫要忘記她曾欺騙她的父親，委身於你；他認為那是妖術——但是我不應再多言，懇請你原諒我對你太過忠心。

奧賽羅：我很感激你的好意。

以阿哥：希望你能明白，我此言乃出於對你的忠愛，但是我驚覺你心神動亂，請求你莫要妄下定論；懷疑是不會使事件成真的。

奧賽羅：我相信黛絲德夢娜是絕對誠實的。

以阿哥：但願她永世不變！也但願你永遠這麼認為！

奧賽羅：但是……

以阿哥：是的，還有另一個重點：自然萬物皆傾向於與自己相似之對象結為夫妻，但是她並未如此。或許能由此般欲望中嗅出一反常態的想法。但是原諒我——我所指的未必是她，雖然我恐怕她在三思之後，可能會拿你和她相同種族的男人們比較，進而拒你於千里之外。

奧賽羅：再見、再見！倘若你再觀察到什麼，務必讓我知道。請尊夫人也多留點心神。現在我想獨處，以阿哥。

以阿哥：閣下，我先行告退。（以阿哥慢慢走開。）

奧賽羅（自言自語）：我為何要結婚？以阿哥是個誠實的人，難怪他會看到與知道更多——多很多——話中還透著弦外之音。

以阿哥（返回）：閣下，稍安勿躁，一切皆未證實。但是你得提防凱西奧，留心尊夫人是否過於積極或頻繁地代他求情；由此便可多瞭解實情。現在就當我的恐懼是愚蠢之舉，認定她是無辜的。

奧賽羅：你大可不必擔心我。

以阿哥：我再次告退。

（以阿哥下。）

奧賽羅：此人非常地誠實，形形色色的人他都瞭解。倘若黛絲德夢娜之事被他說中了，我會將她逐出家門。或許因為我是黑人，抑或許因為我的年紀長於她，她才背叛了我。喔，婚姻是個詛咒，讓我們稱這些可人兒為自己所有，卻又無法控制她們！我寧可化為一隻蟾蜍住在地窖裡，也不願自己珍愛的一部分被別人所占用。喔！黛絲德夢娜來了。（黛絲德夢娜與艾米莉亞再上。）倘若她是虛情假意，那就是上天在嘲笑自己！我是不會相信的。

黛絲德蒙娜：你好嗎，我親愛的奧賽羅？

奧賽羅：我的額頭很痛，這裡。

黛絲德蒙娜：哎呀，想必是因為你的睡眠不夠，讓我將我的手帕綁在你的頭上，如此會有些幫助。

奧賽羅：你的手帕太小了。（他將手帕推開，手帕掉落在地。）別撿了。來吧，我隨你進屋去。

黛絲德蒙娜：我很遺憾你身體不適。

（奧賽羅與黛絲德蒙娜下。）

艾米莉亞（撿起手帕）：我很開心能撿到這個，這是那摩爾人送她的第一份禮物，以阿哥已要求我上百遍要我去偷來。但是她太愛這條手帕以至於隨身攜帶，因奧賽羅要她承諾會永久妥善保管。以阿哥為何想要這個，天曉得，我不得而知，我只是想取悅他。（以阿哥再上。）

以阿哥：你好！你何以獨自在此？

艾米莉亞：我有樣東西要給你——你想要的那條手帕。

以阿哥：是你從她那兒偷來的嗎？

艾米莉亞：當然不是，是她無意間掉了，被我撿到。

以阿哥：好女人！將它交給我。

艾米莉亞：你拿它有何用？

以阿哥（伸手拿）：哎呀，與你何關？

艾米莉亞：倘若未有重要的用途，就將它交還予我，那可憐的夫人發現它遺失了肯定會發瘋的。

以阿哥：莫要透露此事你知情，我自有用途。去吧，你先退下。（艾米莉亞下。）我會將這手帕放在凱西奧的房裡讓他發現；

如此小物甚能説服嫉妒的心，那摩爾人已被我的讒言影響。危險的念頭本質上就是有毒的，初嘗時並不覺得難以入口，但是未幾即會流入血液中，似硫磺一般燒灼。（**奧賽羅再上。**）你好，閣下！

奧賽羅：淫婦！她背著我偷腥，我卻渾然不知？我眼不見、心不想，就於我無傷；我睡得好、吃得飽，就自在而快活。我不知凱西奧那個惡徒早已吻過她，即使全營兵士皆曾與她享受過魚水之歡，我亦快樂如昔——只要我毫不知情。如今我必須向平靜的心靈告別了！向快樂告別！

以阿哥：有此可能嗎，閣下？

奧賽羅：你最好罪證確鑿，以阿哥，給我具體的實證！否則以我永恆的靈魂起誓，你會寧可自己生為一條狗，也不願回應我被喚醒的憤怒！

以阿哥：喔，天啊！喔，願上天寬恕我！喔，駭人的世界！注意啊、注意，世人：直言與誠實可不安全。我感謝你給我這個教訓，從今爾後我不再友愛朋友，因愛會招致此般的斥責。

奧賽羅：不，且慢，你本該誠實。我以全世界起誓，我相信內人的誠實，也疑心她的不忠；我認為你説的是實話，又疑心你所言有虛。我必須見到證據；她的名聲——如黛安娜的臉龐那般純淨無瑕，如今卻似我的面容這般污穢和烏黑。但願我能查到實證！

以阿哥：我明白了，先生，你是被熱情吞噬了，很抱歉我引起了你的疑心。你想要罪證確鑿嗎？

奧賽羅：想要？不，我一定要！

以阿哥：但是要怎麼做？你要如何才能證明，閣下？莫非你想捉姦在床？

奧賽羅：真該死啊！喔！

以阿哥：要現場逮到那姦夫淫婦是很困難的，該怎麼做？

奧賽羅：給我確切的證據，證明她的不忠，我會將她碎屍萬段！

以阿哥：我不喜歡被置於此般處境，但是我就這麼說吧：我聽到凱西奧說了夢話，他說：「甜美的黛絲德夢娜，我們要行事小心，藏好我們的愛！」然後他說：「可恨命運把你許配給那摩爾人！」

奧賽羅：喔，可恨至極！可恨至極！

以阿哥：但這畢竟只是他的夢話。

奧賽羅：即使只是在作夢，還是甚為可疑。

以阿哥：或許這有助於確認其他的證據。告訴我，你是否偶爾見過尊夫人的手裡拿著一條繡著草莓圖樣的手帕？

奧賽羅：怎麼？我給過她一條這樣的手帕，那是我送她的第一份禮物。

以阿哥：這我倒是不知情，但是我今日才見到凱西奧拿這樣的一條手帕在擦抹他的鬍子。

奧賽羅：倘若是同一條手帕——

以阿哥：倘若是同一條手帕，或是屬於她的任何一條，那就是對她不利了，再輔以其他的證據。

奧賽羅：喔，但願她有四萬條性命！一條命太少了，不足以滿足我的復仇之心！如今我能確知此事為真，我對她的愛情已逝。現在你必須幫我，在三日之內讓我聽到你親口說凱西奧已不存在這世上。

以阿哥：就當他已死吧，應允你的所求，但是留她一條活口。

奧賽羅：詛咒她，那邪惡的淫婦！喔，詛咒她！我必須想個速戰速決的方法，殺死那美麗的惡魔。現在由你擔任我的副將。

以阿哥：我願永世為你的奴僕。

（奧賽羅與以阿哥下。）

第三場

P. 072

（黛絲德夢娜與艾米莉亞上，在城堡前面。）

黛絲德夢娜：我會把手帕忘在哪兒了，艾米莉亞？我寧可失去整袋的金幣啊！倘若我那尊貴的摩爾人不是那般理智講理，這就足夠他起疑了。

艾米莉亞：他不是善妒嗎？

黛絲德夢娜：誰，奧賽羅？一點也不！

艾米莉亞：你瞧，他來了。

（奧賽羅上。）

黛絲德夢娜（對奧賽羅）**：**你好嗎，我的夫君？

奧賽羅：我的好夫人。（自言自語：）喔，撒謊竟是如此困難！（對她：）你好嗎，黛絲德夢娜？

黛絲德夢娜：我的夫君，我已差人去找凱西奧來與你相談。

奧賽羅：我嚴重傷風，把你的手帕借給我。

黛絲德夢娜：來，我的夫君。

奧賽羅：我指的是我送你的那條。

黛絲德夢娜：我沒帶在身上。

奧賽羅：可是遺失了？不見了嗎？告訴我，你是否遺忘在某處？

黛絲德夢娜：並未遺失，但萬一遺失了會如何？

奧賽羅：去取來，讓我看看。

黛絲德夢娜：我可以去取，先生，但不是現在，我現在要談談凱西奧，請你將他的職務還給他。

奧賽羅：把手帕給我！

黛絲德夢娜：別這樣！你再也找不到比他更能幹的人。

奧賽羅：手帕！

黛絲德夢娜：求求你，談談凱西奧吧。

奧賽羅：手帕！

黛絲德夢娜：說句實話，你是莫名其妙地不講理。

奧賽羅：離我遠遠的！

（奧賽羅下。）

艾米莉亞：你還說他不善妒？

黛絲德夢娜：我從未見過他如此暴怒！

艾米莉亞：有時候要相處多年才能識得一個男人的真面目。（凱西奧與以阿哥上。）你瞧，是凱西奧和我的夫君！

黛絲德夢娜：凱西奧！你帶來什麼消息？

凱西奧：夫人，還是老樣子，我懇求你找你的夫君相談。

黛絲德夢娜：喔，高尚的凱西奧！我說的話現在也不作數了。我的夫君性情大變，你要有耐心，我必會竭力相助。

以阿哥：我們將軍發怒了嗎？

艾米莉亞：是的，他不知為何似乎心煩意亂，方才匆匆離開。

以阿哥：他怎麼可能發怒？想必是有極其嚴重之事，我去看看。

（以阿哥下。）

黛絲德夢娜（在以阿哥身後喊著）**：**萬事拜託了。（對艾米莉亞：）他必定是為了國務操煩，讓我誤以為他是在我發怒，現在我才驚覺他是為了別的事。

艾米莉亞：祈禱他是因國務而煩亂，而非心生妒忌而發怒。

黛絲德夢娜：我未曾做過對不起他之事！

艾米莉亞：但是妒忌之人不會接受如此的回應，他們的嫉妒未曾有好理由，而是純粹因善妒而嫉妒。那是因妒而生的妖魔，因嫉妒而生出更多的嫉妒。

黛絲德夢娜：願上天驅走奧賽羅心中的這個妖魔！

艾米莉亞：阿們，夫人。

黛絲德夢娜：我這就去找他。來吧，艾米莉亞。

（黛絲德夢娜與艾米莉亞下；畢昂嘉上。）

畢昂嘉：你好，吾友凱西奧，你何以許久未來找我？

凱西奧：我正要去你府上，甜美的畢昂嘉，（將黛絲德夢娜的手帕交予她）你能替我仿作這個刺繡嗎？

畢昂嘉：喔，凱西奧，你這是哪兒來的？是新朋友送你的禮物嗎？我終於知道你為何許久未來找我了。原來如此。

凱西奧：去吧，美麗的姑娘！這不是別的女人送我的。

畢昂嘉：那這是誰的？

凱西奧：我不知道，親愛的，這是我在房裡撿到的，我喜歡這個刺繡圖樣。在失主前來取走之前，我相信必有人前來認領，我想仿作這個圖樣。你拿去繡吧，暫且讓我獨處。

畢昂嘉：讓你獨處？為何？

凱西奧：我在等候將軍，未幾即會去找你。

畢昂嘉：好吧，我靜候你的到來。

（凱西奧與畢昂嘉下。）

第四幕

●第一場

P. 079

（賽浦勒斯，在城堡前面；奧賽羅與以阿哥上。）

以阿哥：你如此以為？

奧賽羅：如此以為，以阿哥？

以阿哥：怎麼，背著旁人親吻？

奧賽羅：禮法不許的一吻。

以阿哥：或是和她朋友赤身裸體在床上超過一個小時，亦無傷大雅？

奧賽羅：赤身裸體在床上，無傷大雅？有如此行徑之人是被惡魔所誘惑，而他們去欺騙天神。

以阿哥：倘若他們未有苟且之事，那就是可寬恕的罪，但倘若我送手帕給我的妻子——

奧賽羅：如何？

以阿哥：哎呀，那就是她的了，閣下。既然是她的，我認為她可以隨意送給任何人。

奧賽羅：她的名譽也是屬於她所有，難道她能隨意送人？

以阿哥：她的名譽是看不見的特質，有些人分明沒有卻看似擁有。但是，至於那條手帕——

奧賽羅：但願我能遺忘此事！然而現在我記得那是在他手上。

以阿哥：是的，那又如何？

奧賽羅：這樣不太妥當。

以阿哥：若是我說我目睹他對你不忠又如何？抑或是我聽見他閒言閒語——

奧賽羅：他說了什麼？

以阿哥：哎呀，就說他——我不知道——躺——

奧賽羅：與她同床？

以阿哥：與她同睡、睡在她身上——隨你怎麼說。

奧賽羅：與她同睡？睡在她身上？天啊，豈有此理！有此可能嗎？喔，惡魔！

（他陷入昏迷。）

以阿哥（竊語）：我的藥物生效了！這輕信他人的傻子已落入圈套，許多高尚貞潔而清白的女人，皆因此而蒙上不白之冤。

（凱西奧上。）

凱西奧：出了什麼事？

以阿哥：我們將軍癲癇發作了。你瞧，他身體在微微顫動。請你暫時回避，待他清醒離開之後，我有事要與你相談，是很重要的事。

（凱西奧下。）

以阿哥（對奧賽羅）：你可安好，將軍？

奧賽羅：不好。他是否認罪？

以阿哥：好閣下，像個男子漢一般接受吧。你並非遭遇此事的第一人。知道真相是比較好的，你不認為嗎？

奧賽羅：喔，你是智者！這是一定的。

以阿哥：你暫且回避。在你昏迷之時，凱西奧來過，我請他先行離開，但是他承諾稍後會再返回。不如你先行躲藏，親眼觀察他臉上的嘲諷和輕蔑？我會讓他再詳加敘述一遍，他在何時何地與尊夫人幽會，且何時會再見面。你只消看他如何回應。

奧賽羅：謝謝你，以阿哥。（奧賽羅躲藏。）

以阿哥（自言自語）：我會問凱西奧關於畢昂嘉之事，她是賣淫賺取麵包糊口和衣服蔽體的風塵女子，而他是她的恩客。她愛凱西奧；妓女一般都會吸引許多男人，但是心中只愛一人。當男人聽聞被她鍾情之時，他必定情不自禁地笑出來。凱西奧來了。（凱西奧上。）當他一微笑，奧賽羅必然發狂。（對凱西奧：）你可安好，副將？

凱西奧：我因被撤職而苦惱萬分，你卻還要這樣稱呼我。

以阿哥：繼續懇求黛絲德夢娜，你必能復職。（壓低聲音說話：）現在，若是讓畢昂嘉來處理此事，你未幾即可恢復職務！

凱西奧：是啊，那可憐的傻丫頭愛我！

奧賽羅：瞧，他已經笑得開懷！

以阿哥：我沒見過如此沉醉愛河中的女人。

凱西奧：那可憐的傻丫頭！

以阿哥：你是否聽聞？她說你會娶她，你是否真有此意？

凱西奧：哈哈哈！娶她——娶個妓女為妻？你可真愛說笑！哈哈哈！她方才還在這兒，我去哪兒她都陰魂不散，我必須擺脫她才行。

以阿哥（聲音壓得很低）：你瞧！她來了。

（畢昂嘉上。）

凱西奧（對畢昂嘉）：你可是在跟蹤我？

畢昂嘉：讓惡魔和他的母親來跟蹤你！你給我那條手帕是何居心？我真是夠傻了才會收下！你說你是在房裡撿到的，不知是誰遺留在那兒？想必是某個輕賤的姑娘吧。拿去！還給你那個婊子，我是不會幫你仿作這個刺繡圖樣的。

凱西奧：究竟怎麼回事，我美麗的畢昂嘉？

奧賽羅：天啊，那是我的手帕！

畢昂嘉：倘若你今晚要上我那兒吃飯，那就來吧；若是不來，就等下回我邀請你時再來。

（畢昂嘉下。）

凱西奧：我還是快點追上去比較好，否則她會當街辱罵我。

以阿哥：你要上她那兒用晚餐嗎？

凱西奧：是的，我確有此意。

以阿哥：那就稍後再見，我真的有事找你相談。

凱西奧：好，稍後再談。

（凱西奧下。）

奧賽羅（從藏身處走出來）：我要殺了他，以阿哥！

以阿哥：你有否見到他對自己的罪行如何一笑置之？你有看到那條手帕嗎？

奧賽羅：我可以花費九年的時間殺死他。優雅的女人！美麗的女人！

以阿哥：不，你必須遺忘那一切。

奧賽羅：是的，今晚就讓她腐爛、死亡、萬劫不復，因她已不容活在世間！不，我的心已化為鐵石。喔，但是那甜美的女人能用歌聲馴服野蠻的熊！她本就有此般溫柔的能力！

以阿哥：是啊，太溫柔了。

奧賽羅：此事已證實，但是可惜了，以阿哥！喔，以阿哥，真是可惜啊！

以阿哥：倘若你那般關愛她，你何不睜一隻眼、閉一隻眼？若是你不介意，他人必定不介意。

奧賽羅：我要將她碎屍萬段！她給我戴了綠帽子——與我的部屬通姦！

以阿哥：那就更可惡了。

奧賽羅：給我一點毒藥，以阿哥，今晚就要！

以阿哥：莫要用毒藥，在她的床上勒死她，就在被她玷污的床上。

奧賽羅：好、好！如此真是大快人心，好極了！

以阿哥：至於凱西奧，就交給我來處理吧，午夜過後便能聽到消息。

（**舞台後方傳來號角聲；羅多維柯、黛絲德夢娜與侍從們上。**）

奧賽羅：那是什麼號角聲？

以阿哥：想必是來自威尼斯之人。是羅多維柯，公爵差遣他來的。瞧，尊夫人亦隨同在側。

羅多維柯：公爵與威尼斯的元老們向你問好。（**他交給奧賽羅一封信。**）

奧賽羅：我親吻此信。（**他拆信閱讀。**）

羅多維柯：副將凱西奧可安好？

以阿哥：他尚健在，先生。

黛絲德夢娜：表親，他和我的夫君起了爭執，但是你必能使他們言歸於好。

奧賽羅：你有把握？

黛絲德夢娜：夫君？

奧賽羅（**讀信**）**：**「務必儘速照辦——」

羅多維柯：他並非在對你説話，而是在忙著讀信。將軍和凱西奧之間是否有歧見？

黛絲德夢娜：很嚴重的糾紛。我希望他們能言好，因我對凱西奧頗有好感。

奧賽羅：真是該死！

黛絲德夢娜：夫君？

羅多維柯：或許是信的內容激怒了他。我猜想他們是要他回國，將他在此地的職務交予凱西奧。

黛絲德夢娜：如此甚好，聞此我心欣喜。

奧賽羅（打她）：惡魔！

黛絲德夢娜（既震驚又驚恐）：我沒做錯事，你不該如此待我。

羅多維柯：閣下，此事若傳回威尼斯必定無人相信，即便我親眼目睹亦難以置信。快向她賠罪，她哭了。

奧賽羅：喔，惡魔、惡魔！倘若女人的淚水能在土地上播種，那她的每滴眼淚都將化成鱷魚！滾出我的視線！

黛絲德夢娜：我不會留在這兒惹你不悅。

（因震驚而虛弱的她，轉身離開。）

奧賽羅：你走！我稍後再差人去找你。（黛絲德夢娜下，淚流滿面。）（對羅多維科，憤怒地：）先生，我會服從此信的內容，返回威尼斯，讓凱西奧代理我的職務！還有，先生，今晚希望我們能共進晚餐，歡迎你來到賽浦勒斯。（他鞠躬，然後怒氣沖沖地離開。）這些好色之徒！

羅多維柯：這是我們元老院所看重的那尊貴的摩爾人嗎？泰山崩於前而面不改色的那個人？

以阿哥：他性情大變。

羅多維柯：他的神志清楚嗎？他瘋了嗎？

以阿哥：他現在是你眼中看到的這樣，但願他能回復以前的模樣！

羅多維柯：他毆打他的妻子？

以阿哥：哎呀！此舉確實不妥，恐怕他還有更惡劣之行徑。

羅多維柯：他平常即是如此？抑或是那封信激怒了他？

以阿哥：哎呀、哎呀！我不該透露我曾親眼目睹的事。你還是親自觀察吧。

羅多維柯：很遺憾我先前錯看了他。

（全體下。）

第二場

P. 090

（城堡內的一個房間；奧賽羅與艾米莉亞上。）

奧賽羅：所以你什麼也沒看見？

艾米莉亞：亦不曾聽見或懷疑什麼。

奧賽羅：但是你見過她和凱西奧在一起？

艾米莉亞：是的，但我並未見到不妥之言行；他們的對話內容我都聽得一清二楚。

奧賽羅：怎麼——他們難道未曾低聲耳語？

艾米莉亞：從未，閣下。

奧賽羅：也未曾打發你回避？

艾米莉亞：從未！

奧賽羅：那就奇怪了。

艾米莉亞：閣下，我願以靈魂擔保她的忠貞，你莫要有所疑心！倘若有哪個惡徒給你此般的念頭，但願上天懲罰他。倘若她有不忠、不貞或不誠實之處，這世上必無快樂的男人。

奧賽羅：請她來此找我，去吧。（艾米莉亞下。）她說得好聽，但是再愚笨的婦人也可能編出此般謊言。

（黛絲德夢娜與艾米莉亞上。）

黛絲德夢娜：我的夫君，你有何吩咐？

奧賽羅：讓我看看你的眼睛，看著我。

黛絲德夢娜：你究竟有何可怕的念頭？

奧賽羅（對艾米莉亞）**：**你暫且回避，關上門。

（艾米莉亞下。）

奧賽羅：告訴我，你是什麼？

黛絲德夢娜：你的妻子，夫君，你誠實又忠貞的妻子。

奧賽羅：過來，為你的誠實發誓。

黛絲德夢娜：上天明白我的誠實！

奧賽羅：上天知道你虛偽如惡魔。

黛絲德夢娜：什麼？對誰虛偽，夫君？與誰虛偽？我如何虛偽？

奧賽羅：啊，黛絲德夢娜！你走吧！你走！

黛絲德夢娜：喔，如此悲傷的一天！你為何哭泣？你的眼淚是因我而流的嗎，夫君？你懷疑召你回威尼斯是我父親的提議嗎？莫要因此而怪罪於我。

奧賽羅：倘若上天賜我一些病痛，或是使我一貧如洗，抑或是使我淪為奴隸，或許我皆可承受，但是要將我逐出我心靈的歸宿——我便有如墮入地獄一般啊！

黛絲德夢娜：我尊貴的夫君，祈望你知道我的忠貞。

奧賽羅：我倒寧願你未曾出生過！

黛絲德夢娜：哎呀！我究竟犯了什麼罪而不自知？

奧賽羅：你犯了什麼罪？你這無恥的淫婦！

黛絲德夢娜：天啊，你冤枉我了。

奧賽羅：難道你不是淫婦？

黛絲德夢娜：不是，我以基督徒的身分向你發誓！

奧賽羅：怎麼——你不是娼妓？

黛絲德夢娜：不是！我願對天發誓。

奧賽羅：有此可能嗎？

黛絲德夢娜：喔，願上天幫助我們！

奧賽羅：那我請求你的寬恕，我誤以為你是嫁給奧賽羅的那位狡猾威尼斯娼妓。（**大喊：**）過來這兒，女人！（**艾米莉亞上。**）你的使命與聖彼得恰巧相反，你這看守地獄之門的女人！你，就是你！（**給她錢。**）我們談完了，這是勞煩你的賠罪賞錢，我們會面之事請你保密。

（**奧賽羅下。**）

艾米莉亞：天啊，他在想什麼？你可安好，我的好夫人？

黛絲德夢娜：坦白說，我甚為震驚，哭不出眼淚，也說不出半句不該含淚說出的話。用我新婚的床單為我鋪床吧，請你的夫君前來此處。

艾米莉亞：果真情勢驟變！

（艾米莉亞下。）

黛絲德夢娜：但願上天憐憫我！我做了什麼使他認定我的不貞？

（以阿哥與艾米莉亞上。）

以阿哥：我能為你效勞嗎，夫人？

黛絲德夢娜：我也不確定。

以阿哥：怎麼了，夫人？

艾米莉亞：哎呀，以阿哥，將軍無情地罵她是娼妓。

以阿哥：他何以如此？

黛絲德夢娜：我不知道。

以阿哥：莫要哭泣！真是悲傷的一天！

艾米莉亞：難道她拒絕了許多名門貴族的求婚，拋下了父親、國家和朋友們，卻落得娼妓之名嗎？難道她無權哭泣？

以阿哥：他要為此受到詛咒！他何以這麼說？

黛絲德夢娜：唯有天知道。

艾米莉亞：必定是有某個惡徒、某個騙人的無賴，撒了這個漫天大謊。倘若我說錯，你大可以絞死我。

以阿哥：沒有這樣的人，這是不可能的事。

黛絲德夢娜：倘若有，但願上天寬恕他！

艾米莉亞：讓絞刑套索去寬恕他吧！但願地獄啃噬他的骨頭！何以有人會罵她是娼妓？那摩爾人是被惡徒所誤導。

以阿哥：說話要小心一點。

艾米莉亞：喔，詛咒他下地獄！那種人甚至會讓你以為我是那摩爾人的情婦！

以阿哥：你這傻子，要謹言慎行。

黛絲德夢娜：以阿哥，好友，你去勸他。告訴你，我是真心愛他，他的無情可能毀了我的一生，但是永遠改變不了我的愛。

以阿哥：莫要苦惱，他只是一時情緒使然。國務使他憤怒，他將怒氣發洩在你身上，如此而已，我向你保證。（**後台傳來號角聲。**）聽，號角聲在召喚你去用晚餐了！進去吧，莫再哭泣，一切皆會好轉。（**黛絲德夢娜與艾米莉亞下；羅德里戈上。**）你好，羅德里戈！

羅德里戈：你一直在欺騙我，先生。

以阿哥：何出此言？

羅德里戈：你一直敷衍搪塞我，以阿哥，我所有的錢財都揮霍殆盡。我委請你轉交給黛絲德夢娜的珠寶首飾，也足夠動搖一個修女的貪念了，你說她已然收受，你引導我燃起接近她的希望，然而一切都並未發生。

以阿哥：稍安勿躁，一切都好。

羅德里戈：不，一切都不好！事實上，我開始覺得你不值得信賴。我會親自向黛絲德夢娜表白；倘若她願意退回我餽贈的珠寶，我會和她保持距離，否則我必定要你付出代價。

以阿哥：看來你畢竟有點骨氣。你的憤怒乃是合乎情理！但是我仍要向你保證，我向來對你公正無二。

羅德里戈：看起來並非如此。

以阿哥：這我承認，你的疑慮並非空穴來風。但是羅德里戈，我此刻比從前更相信你有決心、勇氣和膽量。今晚就展現出來吧！倘若黛絲德夢娜明晚仍不屬於你，就以叛逆罪使我從這世上消失！

羅德里戈：你有何計畫？是否合理與可行？

以阿哥：先生，威尼斯傳來正式的命令，任命凱西奧取代奧賽羅的職務。

羅德里戈：真有此事？那奧賽羅和黛絲德夢娜即將返回威尼斯。

以阿哥：喔，不，他要前去茅利塔尼亞，帶著黛絲德夢娜同行，除非發生意外迫使他留在此地。除掉凱西奧就能迫使此一結果發生。

羅德里戈：除掉他？你此言何意？

以阿哥：就是使他無法接手奧賽羅的職務——打破他的腦袋。

羅德里戈：這是你要我做的事？

以阿哥：是的——倘若你有膽量做出對你最有好處之事。凱西奧今晚要和一名娼妓共進晚餐，我會去那兒找他，他尚不知自己好運臨頭。倘若你留心等候他離開的時機，你就能隨時解決他，我會就近支援你。此事不得告訴第三人，他必死無疑。莫要神情如此驚恐，但請你隨我來。

羅德里戈：我想多聽聽此一計畫的理由。

以阿哥：你會聽到的！

（羅德里戈與以阿哥下。）

●第三場 P. 099

（城堡內的另一個房間。奧賽羅、羅多維柯、黛絲德夢娜、艾米莉亞與侍從們上。）

奧賽羅（對羅多維柯）：陪我散散步，先生？（對黛絲德夢娜：）你先行就寢，我未幾即會返家，現在就打發你的僕人退下，切記要做到。

黛絲德夢娜：我會的，夫君。

（奧賽羅、羅多維柯與侍從們下。）

艾米莉亞：他似乎心情好了許多。

黛絲德夢娜：他說他未幾即會返家，他要我先行就寢，還要我打發你退下。

艾米莉亞：什麼？打發我退下？

黛絲德夢娜：那是他的囑咐，所以艾米莉亞，將我的睡袍交予我，再見了，此刻莫要再惹他不悅。

艾米莉亞：但願你未曾認識他！

黛絲德夢娜：但這非我所願，我是真心愛他。

艾米莉亞（幫她更衣準備就寢）：我鋪床時已換成你要求的床單。

黛絲德夢娜：無所謂了。我的老天，我們可真傻！倘若我先你一步離世，請你用這床單包裹我的遺體。

艾米莉亞：好了啦！你說這是什麼傻話？

黛絲德夢娜：喔，這些男人！這些男人！你真的認為——告訴我，艾米莉亞——世上真有對丈夫不忠的女人嗎？

艾米莉亞：是有一些，這是無庸置疑的。

黛絲德夢娜：你願為全世界的財富而不忠嗎？

艾米莉亞：哎呀——難道你不會？

黛絲德夢娜：不，我以滿天的星光起誓，我絕不會！

艾米莉亞：我是不會以星光起誓的，在黑暗中要偷情更是容易。

黛絲德夢娜：你果真願為全世界的財富而不忠？

艾米莉亞：世界如此之大，犯點小惡能得此財富乃莫大的報酬。

黛絲德夢娜：相信你絕無此意！

艾米莉亞：我有，我會在做了之後再行彌補過錯。想當然爾，我不會為了一枚小戒指，或是為了房產，抑或是洋裝、禮服或帽子，或是任何小禮物而做這樣的事。但是為了全世界的財富？我的老天！誰不願出賣貞操而讓自己的丈夫登基為王？

黛絲德夢娜：倘若我做出如此行徑，即便是為了全世界的財富，也一樣要詛咒我！

艾米莉亞：哎呀，那只是世上諸多錯誤之一！倘若你做了一件錯事能換得全世界的財富，那就是在你自己的世界犯錯，你未幾即可再重新導正一切過錯。

黛絲德夢娜：我並不認為世上有那樣的女人！

艾米莉亞：這種女人多到足夠填滿全世界！但我覺得妻子們

做錯了事，就是她們丈夫的過錯。假若他們將我們珍愛之物送予其他女人，或是無端心生醋意，對我們呼之即來、揮之即去，或者假使他們毆打我們——哎呀，我們亦會發怒！甚至我們會有復仇之心。妻子們也和丈夫們一樣有感情，亦如她們的丈夫一般能看見、嗅到和嘗得酸甜苦辣。他們何以拒絕我們另覓新歡？只為逢場作戲？或許是吧。此乃慾望使然？應該是。他們是因意志不堅而犯罪？那是當然。難道我們不像男人們那樣，也有渴望、情慾和意志不堅嗎？讓他們善待我們吧——或是讓他們知道我們也會有他們那般的行徑，事實如此。

黛絲德夢娜：晚安、晚安，但願上天教我莫要以怨報怨，而是從中記取教訓！

（黛絲德夢娜與艾米莉亞下。）

第五幕

●第一場

P. 105

（在賽浦勒斯的一條街道；以阿哥與羅德里戈上。）

以阿哥：他未幾即會前來，羅德里戈，你的劍先出鞘吧，隨時準備使用。快、快！莫要害怕，我會就近協助。

羅德里戈：別走遠了，我可能會出差錯。

以阿哥：我就在這兒，拿出膽量！

（以阿哥躲藏起來。）

羅德里戈：此事我並不確定，但是他給了我下手的好理由。只是取走另一個人的性命，我的劍準備就緒！他非死不可！

以阿哥（竊語）：好極了，我已激起這年輕小伙子的決心，如今他愈來愈憤怒，無論是他殺死凱西奧，或是凱西奧殺死他，或是他倆相互殘殺，我皆能坐收漁翁之利。倘若羅德里戈活著，他會要我歸還我違背他所託、未轉交予黛絲德夢娜的所有黃金和珠寶；此事千萬不得發生。倘若凱西奧活著，那摩爾人可能會將我的謊言洩露予他，那會置我於非常危險之境地——所以他必須死！我聽到他過來了。

（凱西奧上。）

羅德里戈：我認得他走路的模樣，是凱西奧！惡徒，準備受死！

（羅德里戈持劍攻擊凱西奧，但是未能傷他。凱西奧拔劍重傷了羅德里戈。）

羅德里戈：喔，我被殺了！

（以阿哥刺傷凱西奧的腿，迅速下。）

凱西奧：我的腿被廢了！救命啊！殺人！殺人！（他倒下。）

（奧賽羅上。）

奧賽羅（自言自語）：那是凱西奧！以阿哥兑現了承諾。喔，勇敢的以阿哥！他對被苛待的朋友果真講義氣。他給我上了一課！好了，蕩婦，你的情人已死，你的死期亦將至。我這就來了，淫婦，我已將你的魅惑從我心上抹除，你沾染姦情的床上，未幾即將沾上你淫蕩的鮮血。

（奧賽羅下；羅多維柯與葛拉提安諾上。）

凱西奧：救命啊！沒人經過嗎？殺人！

葛拉提安諾：好淒厲的哭喊聲！

凱西奧：喔，救我！

羅多維柯：你聽！天色如此昏暗，我看不清。

羅德里戈：喔，卑鄙的惡徒！沒人伸出援手嗎？那我要失血過多而亡了。

（**以阿哥上，手持一把火炬。**）

以阿哥：我是否聽見哭喊聲？

凱西奧：這裡、這裡！看在老天的份上，救我！

以阿哥：怎麼了？

凱西奧：以阿哥？在這兒！我被惡徒所傷！

以阿哥：喔，不，副將！是誰傷了你？

凱西奧：其中一人應該還在附近，無法跑遠。

以阿哥：喔，那些該死的叛徒！（**對羅多維柯與葛拉提安諾：**）來者何人？快來幫我的忙。

羅德里戈：喔，幫幫我！

凱西奧：那就是其中一位兇手。

以阿哥（對羅德里戈）：你這殺人兇手！你這惡徒！（以阿哥刺死羅德里戈。）

羅德里戈：喔，該死的以阿哥！你這沒人性的狗！（羅德里戈死去。）

以阿哥：竟然想到要摸黑殺人！這些嗜血的惡賊何在？這個城鎮好安靜！喂！殺人了！殺人！（對羅多維柯與葛拉提安諾：）你們是何人？是友或敵？

羅多維柯：從我們的言行即可判知。

以阿哥：羅多維柯先生？

羅多維柯：是的，先生。

以阿哥：抱歉有所得罪。這是凱西奧，他遭到惡徒們的攻擊。

葛拉提安諾：凱西奧！

以阿哥：你可安好，弟兄？

凱西奧：我的腿傷嚴重。

以阿哥：我用我的上衣為你包紮傷口。

（畢昂嘉上。）

畢昂嘉（看到凱西奧）：喔，凱西奧！我親愛的凱西奧！喔，凱西奧、凱西奧！

以阿哥：各位，我懷疑他的傷和這個蕩婦有關。（手持火炬照向羅德里戈。）我們認識這個人嗎？哎呀，是我親愛的朋友羅德里戈！這不可能，但是事實擺在眼前。天啊！羅德里戈！（對凱西奧：）你倆究竟有何仇恨？

凱西奧：沒有，我甚至不認識他。

以阿哥（**對畢昂嘉**）**：**哎呀，你的臉色如此蒼白，你眼神中的恐懼暗示著內疚。（**對其他人：**）將他們抬走，我會差遣醫生為凱西奧療傷。

（**凱西奧與羅德里戈被人抬下；艾米莉亞上。**）

艾米莉亞：怎麼了，夫君？

以阿哥：凱西奧在黑暗中於此地被羅德里戈等人攻擊，其他人皆已逃跑。他差點送了命，羅德里戈已死。

艾米莉亞：喔，哎呀，好凱西奧！

以阿哥：此即為娼賣淫的下場。艾米莉亞，請你去問問凱西奧他今晚在哪兒用膳。（**對畢昂嘉：**）怎麼？我的疑問使你顫抖嗎？

畢昂嘉：他是在我的住處用晚餐——但是我並非因此而顫抖。

以阿哥：喔，是嗎？我命令你，隨我來。

艾米莉亞：詛咒你，娼婦！

畢昂嘉：我不是娼婦，我如同指控我的任何人一般誠實。

艾米莉亞：胡扯！詛咒你！

以阿哥：我們去找醫生為凱西奧療傷。（**對畢昂嘉：**）走吧，女人，你最好想出另一套說詞。艾米莉亞，快快前往城堡，將在此發生之事告知將軍和夫人。快去！

（**他們下。**）

●第二場

P. 111

（黛絲德夢娜在城堡內的臥房內熟睡；奧賽羅手持蠟燭上。）

奧賽羅：我既不會讓她濺血，亦不會在她那比雪更白的皮膚上留疤，但是她必須死，否則她會背叛更多男人。我先滅了這燭光，再滅了她生命的火光。（他親吻她。）她甜美的氣息幾乎要説服我饒她不死。再一吻，再一次！這是最後一次！這甜美從未曾如此致命。我必須啜泣，但這是殘酷的淚水，我的悲傷宛如上帝在懲罰祂深愛之罪人時的愁苦。她要醒來了。

黛絲德夢娜：來者何人？奧賽羅？

奧賽羅：是的，黛絲德夢娜。

黛絲德夢娜：你要就寢了嗎，我的夫君？

奧賽羅：你今晚有否禱告？

黛絲德夢娜：有的，夫君。

奧賽羅：你能想到先前尚未向上天告解的任何罪嗎？若是有，現在就請求赦免吧，我不想殺死你未準備好的靈魂？

黛絲德夢娜：什麼？你提到殺死嗎？

奧賽羅：是的。

黛絲德夢娜：那就願上帝對我慈悲！

奧賽羅：想想你的罪。

黛絲德夢娜：我的罪就是我對你的所有的愛。

奧賽羅：是的，為此你必須死。

黛絲德夢娜：因愛而殺人乃違反常理之事，究竟怎麼回事？

奧賽羅：我送你的那條手帕——你送給了凱西奧。

黛絲德夢娜：不，我以我的生命和靈魂起誓，我此生未曾待你不忠！我對凱西奧僅止於朋友之愛，我未曾送他愛的信物。

奧賽羅：我看到我的手帕在他的手裡，你這滿口謊言的女人！你將我的心化為鐵石，你使我稱我將做之事為謀殺，而我只視之為犧牲。我看到那條手帕了！

黛絲德夢娜：那想必是他撿到的，我從未曾贈予他。去找他來，讓他坦承真相。

奧賽羅：他已坦承不諱。

黛絲德夢娜：坦承什麼，夫君？

奧賽羅：坦承他與你有染。

黛絲德夢娜：怎麼會？不忠之情？

奧賽羅：是的。

黛絲德夢娜：他不會這麼說的。

奧賽羅：的確不會，他已被封口，我下令誠實的以阿哥前去解決他。

黛絲德夢娜：什麼——他死了嗎？

奧賽羅：即便他的每根頭髮都有生命，我的復仇之心亦早已將之摧毀殆盡。

黛絲德夢娜：天啊！他遭人陷害，而我亦將斷送性命。

奧賽羅：夠了，淫婦！你竟當著我的面為他哭泣？

黛絲德夢娜：喔，驅逐我吧，夫君，但求你別殺死我！

奧賽羅：你死吧，淫婦！

黛絲德夢娜：再讓我禱告一次！

奧賽羅：為時已晚！

（奧賽羅悶死黛絲德夢娜。）

艾米莉亞（在門外）：將軍、將軍！

奧賽羅（還在悶死黛絲德夢娜，她在掙扎）：這是什麼聲音？還沒死嗎？我或許殘酷，但是我亦有惻隱之心，我不會讓你痛苦太久，快解脫了。

艾米莉亞（從舞台後方）：將軍、將軍！我有事向你稟報！

奧賽羅（對艾米莉亞）：好、好，請稍候片刻！（自言自語：）是艾米莉亞，她可能是來通報凱西奧的死訊。（看著黛絲德夢娜：）一動也不動了？如同一具死屍。我是否該讓那丫鬟進來？這可是明智之舉？她似乎又動了，該怎麼做才最好？倘若那丫鬟進來了，她會想和我的妻子說話。我的妻子！什麼妻子？我沒有妻子！喔，簡直令人難以承受！喔，沉重的時刻！

艾米莉亞：讓我和你相談，將軍！

奧賽羅：我這就出去！（自言自語：）讓我先拉上床邊的窗簾。（開門：）怎麼了？

艾米莉亞：喔，我的好將軍，有人犯下可憎的命案！凱西奧殺死了一名年輕的威尼斯人，名喚羅德里戈。

奧賽羅：羅德里戈被人殺死？那凱西奧呢？

艾米莉亞：不，凱西奧並未死。

奧賽羅：凱西奧並未死？那就是殺錯人了，我美好的復仇計畫生變了。

黛絲德夢娜（虛弱地）**：**錯了，殺錯人了！

艾米莉亞：喔，將軍，那個是什麼聲音？

奧賽羅：哪個？什麼？

艾米莉亞：喔，不！那是我家夫人的聲音。（**拉開床邊的窗簾：**）救命啊！救命！喔，夫人，再說說話啊！甜美的黛絲德夢娜！喔，親愛的夫人，說話啊！

黛絲德夢娜：我清白無罪卻要死去。

艾米莉亞：喔，是誰如此痛下殺手？

黛絲德夢娜：沒有誰，是我自己。再見了，代我向我善良的夫君美言幾句。喔，永別了！（**她死去。**）

奧賽羅：是我殺死了她。

艾米莉亞：喔，那她就更是聖潔如同天使，而你則是邪惡的魔鬼！

奧賽羅：她對我不忠，她是個淫婦。

艾米莉亞：你冤枉了她，你這惡魔！她如同天使一般忠貞！

奧賽羅：凱西奧與她相姦，你丈夫知曉所有的實情。

艾米莉亞：我丈夫？

奧賽羅：你丈夫。

艾米莉亞：說她違背了她的婚誓？

奧賽羅：是的，與凱西奧偷情。

艾米莉亞：我丈夫！

奧賽羅：你何以不斷重複同一句話，女人？我就說是你丈夫，我的朋友、你的丈夫，誠實的以阿哥。

艾米莉亞：倘若他這麼說，但願他邪惡的靈魂日漸腐爛！他滿口胡言，她對這骯髒的婚姻是心滿意足，你此舉是天理難容，亦使你配不上她。

奧賽羅：哼！你還是閉嘴吧。

艾米莉亞：你這傻子！愚蠢至極！你如泥土一般無知！即使你殺死我二十條命，我也要去告發你。救命啊！救命！來人啊，救命！那摩爾人殺死了我家夫人！殺人了！

（蒙塔諾、葛拉提安諾、以阿哥與其他人上。）

蒙塔諾：怎麼了？

艾米莉亞：喔，你也來了，以阿哥？你幹的好事，讓別的男人將他們的殺人罪行栽到你的頭上。證明這惡徒是錯的——倘若你是個男人。他說你告訴他其妻不貞，我知道你不會這麼說，你沒那般歹毒。說吧，因我心已痛苦不堪。

以阿哥：我將我疑心之事告訴他，是他自己信以為真。

艾米莉亞：但你是否曾説過她不貞？

以阿哥：我是説過。

艾米莉亞：你説謊，萬惡不赦的漫天大謊！她——和凱西奧私通？你是説凱西奧嗎？

以阿哥：和凱西奧私通，女人，請你冷靜。

艾米莉亞：我不會冷靜，我不吐不快！我家夫人躺在這兒，在她的床上被人殺害——

全體：喔，不會吧！

艾米莉亞：是因為你的話，以阿哥，才招致了這場命案。

奧賽羅：別再瞠目凝視了，各位，木已成舟。

葛拉提安諾：太可怕了！

蒙塔諾：野蠻獸行！

艾米莉亞：可惡、殘暴、太邪惡了！我要出於哀傷而自盡了！

以阿哥：你瘋了嗎？我命令你回家去。

艾米莉亞：或許，以阿哥，我將永遠不再回家。

奧賽羅：喔！喔！喔！（他倒臥在床上。）

艾米莉亞：儘管躺那兒哭喊吧！因你殺死了世上最甜美無辜之人。

奧賽羅（起身）**：**喔，她是蛇蠍心腸！很是遺憾，但以阿哥知道她和凱西奧犯下這恬不知恥之罪行已有上千次，她甚至在相姦之後還將我初次贈予她的定情之物轉送給他。我看到他手裡拿著那條手帕——那是當年家父贈與家母的禮物。

艾米莉亞：喔，天啊！喔，天上的父啊！

以阿哥：夠了，安靜！

艾米莉亞：我要如北風一般自由地說話。喔，你這愚蠢的摩爾人！那條手帕是我無意間撿到的，交給了我的丈夫，因他經常認真地懇求我偷來給他。

以阿哥：你這惡毒的婦人！

艾米莉亞：她送給了凱西奧？不，是我撿到的——而我交給了我丈夫。

以阿哥：你這齷齪的東西，滿口謊言！

艾米莉亞：我對天發誓，我沒撒謊，各位。（對奧賽羅：）你這殺人的蠢貨！何以如此愚蠢之人會有這般良善的妻子？

（奧賽羅攻擊以阿哥，但是被蒙塔諾所阻止。以阿哥用他的劍刺向艾米莉亞。）

葛拉提安諾：他殺死了他的妻子。

艾米莉亞：是啊，讓我躺在我家夫人的身旁。

（以阿哥下。）

葛拉提安諾：他跑了，但是他的妻子已然遇害。

蒙塔諾：好個惡徒！用我方才從那摩爾人手中奪下的這個武器，守住外面的門；倘若他意圖離開，殺了他。我去追捕以阿哥，因他是該死的無賴。

（蒙塔諾與葛拉提安諾下，獨留奧賽羅與艾米莉亞。）

奧賽羅：我似乎失去了我的勇氣，此刻任何怯懦之人皆可奪下我的劍！然而何以我的榮譽仍在？讓我失去一切吧。

艾米莉亞：摩爾人，她守身如玉。她愛你啊，殘酷的摩爾人，我所言句句實屬——我要死了。（她死去。）

奧賽羅：我在這房內還有另一把劍。喔，在這兒。（**向屋外呼喊：**）叔父，我必須出去！

葛拉提安諾（**從舞台後方**）**：**若你膽敢嘗試，就要你付出極大的代價。你沒有武器，毫無勝算。

奧賽羅：那就進來吧，陪我說話，否則我即使手無寸鐵也會攻擊。

（**葛拉提安諾上。**）

葛拉提安諾：怎麼了？

奧賽羅：你瞧，我確有武器。莫要害怕，此乃我人生旅程的終點。（**對黛絲德夢娜：**）你此刻何如？喔，命運多舛的女人！蒼白如你的睡袍一般！冰冷、冰冷啊，我的姑娘！一如你的美德。喔，我真是個該被詛咒的傻瓜！鞭笞我吧，你們這些惡魔，將這絕美的景象從我心頭抹去！在流動的火坑裡洗淨我！喔，黛絲德夢娜！死了，黛絲德夢娜！死了！喔！喔！喔！

（**羅多維柯、蒙塔諾、坐在椅子上被抬著的凱西奧與軍官上，押著被逮捕收押的以阿哥。**）

羅多維柯：這不幸的莽夫何在？

奧賽羅：從前的奧賽羅嗎？在這兒。（**對以阿哥：**）你這惡魔！（**他持劍刺向以阿哥。**）

羅多維柯：奪下他手裡的劍！

（**奧賽羅被奪劍。**）

以阿哥：我在流血，先生，但是並未被殺死。

奧賽羅：我並不後悔，我寧可你活著，因在我看來，死了才是幸福。

羅多維柯：是你和他共謀殺死凱西奧嗎？

奧賽羅：是的。

凱西奧：親愛的將軍，你沒理由殺我啊。

奧賽羅：我相信你，也請求你的寬恕！問問以阿哥他為何誘騙我犯下此罪。

以阿哥：莫要問我，我不再開口說話。

奧賽羅（對以阿哥）**：**你這可惡的懦夫。凱西奧，你是如何得到我妻子的那條手帕？

凱西奧：我在房裡撿到的。以阿哥坦承是他蓄意將之留在我房內，只為了實現他的計畫。

奧賽羅：喔，我真是愚蠢！愚蠢！愚蠢！

凱西奧：我們找到羅德里戈的一封親筆信，他指控以阿哥逼迫他在我守夜之時引我上勾，致使我遭到解職。所以即便他已死亡多時，此刻仍有話可說。以阿哥毀了他，是以阿哥引導他誤入歧途。

羅多維柯（對奧賽羅）**：**隨我們來，你的權力和軍權皆被撤除，從今爾後由凱西奧統治賽浦勒斯。至於以阿哥——倘若有任何酷刑能給他極大的痛苦，那就施用在他的身上吧。你將被監禁，嚴加看守，直到你的罪行傳遍威尼斯各地。來，我們走吧。

奧賽羅：且慢！在你們離開前我有幾句話要說。我懇求你們，當你們陳述此事之時，就說我是用情太深，只是愛得不甚明智；我不會輕易生妒，只是一旦被煽動就會困惑不已；我親手丟棄了價值高於全國人民的一顆珍珠。這一切全都寫下來！也記下曾經有個歹毒的土耳其人，裹著頭巾攻擊一名威尼斯人，誹謗我國，我扼住那條狗的喉嚨殺了他——就像這樣。（他取出暗藏的一把刀子刺向自己。）

羅多維柯：喔，如此血腥的結局！

奧賽羅（對黛絲德夢娜）：我在殺死你之前親吻了你，如今除此之外別無他法，唯有自盡一途，以這一吻了結殘生。

（倒臥在床上，親吻她，然後死去。）

羅多維柯（對以阿哥）：喔，你這隻惡犬！瞧瞧這床上的血腥慘狀，全是你的傑作。此情此景著實悽慘，還是遮掩為宜。（對葛拉提安諾：）葛拉提安諾，守好這個屋子，取走那摩爾人的財產，因你是他的繼承人。（對凱西奧：）總督閣下，確保這心腸歹毒的惡徒受到懲罰，現在是你的職責。我即刻要啟程了，懷著沉重的心情，回國稟告這些不幸的事件。

（全體下。）

Literary Glossary • 文學詞彙表

aside 竊語

一種台詞。演員在台上講此台詞時，其他角色是聽不見的。角色通常藉由竊語來向觀眾抒發內心感受。

- Although she appeared to be calm, the heroine's **aside** revealed her inner terror.
  雖然女主角看似冷靜，但她的**竊語**透露出她內在的恐懼。

backstage 後台

一個戲院空間。演員都在此處準備上台，舞台布景也存放此處。

- Before entering, the villain impatiently waited **backstage**.
  在上台前，壞人在**後台**焦躁地等待。

cast 演員；卡司陣容

戲劇的全體演出人員。

- The entire **cast** must attend tonight's dress rehearsal.
  全體演員必須參加今晚的正式排練。

character 角色

故事或戲劇中虛構的人物。

- Mighty Mouse is one of my favorite cartoon **characters**.
  太空飛鼠是我最愛的卡通**人物**之一。

climax 劇情高峰

戲劇或小說中主要衝突的結局。

- The outlaw's capture made an exciting **climax** to the story.
  逃犯落網成為故事中最刺激的**精彩情節**。

comedy 喜劇

有趣好笑的戲劇、電影和電視劇，並有快樂完美的結局。

■ My friends and I always enjoy a Jim Carrey **comedy**.
我朋友和我總是很喜歡金凱瑞演的**喜劇**。

conflict 戲劇衝突

故事主要的角色較量、勢力對抗或想法衝突。

■ *Dr. Jekyll and Mr. Hyde* illustrates the **conflict** between good and evil.
《變身怪醫》描述善惡之間的**衝突**。

conclusion 尾聲

解決情節衝突的方法，使故事結束。

■ That play's **conclusion** was very satisfying. Every conflict was resolved. 該劇的**結局**十分令人滿意，所有的衝突都被圓滿解決。

dialogue 對白

小說或戲劇角色所說的話語。

■ Amusing **dialogue** is an important element of most comedies.
有趣的**對白**是大多喜劇中一項重要的元素。

drama 戲劇

故事，通常非喜劇類型，特別是寫來讓演員在戲劇或電影中演出。

■ The TV **drama** about spies was very suspenseful.
那齣關於間諜的電視**劇**非常懸疑。

event 事件

發生的事情；特別的事。

■ The most exciting **event** in the story was the surprise ending.
故事中最精彩的**事件**是意外的結局。

introduction 簡介

一篇簡短的文章，呈現並解釋小說或戲劇的劇情。

■ The **introduction** to *Frankenstein* is in the form of a letter.
《科學怪人》的**簡介**是以信件的型式呈現。

motive 動機

一股內在或外在的力量，迫使角色做出某些事情。

■ What was that character's **motive** for telling a lie?
那個角色說謊的**動機**為何？

passage 段落

書寫作品的部分內容，範圍短至一行，長至幾段。

■ His favorite **passage** from the book described the author's childhood.
他在書中最喜歡的**段落**描述了該作者的童年。

playwright 劇作家

戲劇的作者。

■ William Shakespeare is the world's most famous **playwright**.
威廉莎士比亞是世界上最知名的**劇作家**。

plot 情節

故事或戲劇中一連串的因果事件，導致最終結局。

■ The **plot** of that mystery story is filled with action.
該推理故事的**情節**充滿打鬥。

point of view 觀點

由角色的心理層面來看待故事發展的狀況。

■ The father's **point of view** about elopement was quite different from the daughter's. 父親對於私奔的**看法**與女兒迥然不同。

prologue 序幕

在戲劇第一幕開始前的介紹。

- The playwright described the main characters in the **prologue** to the play.
  劇作家在**序幕**中描述了主要角色。

quotation 名句

被引述的文句；某角色所說的詞語；在引號內的文字。

- A popular **quotation** from *Julius Caesar* begins, "Friends, Romans, countrymen . . ."
  《凱薩大帝》中常被**引用的文句**開頭是：「各位朋友，各位羅馬人，各位同胞……」。

role 角色

演員在劇中揣摩表演的人物。

- Who would you like to see play the **role** of Romeo?
  你想看誰飾演羅密歐這個**角色**呢？

sequence 順序

故事或事件發生的時序。

- Sometimes actors rehearse their scenes out of **sequence**.
  演員有時會不按**順序**排練他們出場的戲。

setting 情節背景

故事發生的地點與時間。

- This play's **setting** is New York in the 1940s.
  戲劇的**背景設定**於 1940 年代的紐約。

soliloquy 獨白

角色向觀眾發表想法的一番言論，猶如自言自語。

- One famous **soliloquy** is Hamlet's speech that begins, "To be, or not to be . . ."
  哈姆雷特最知名的**獨白**是：「生，抑或是死……」。

symbol 象徵

用以代表其他事物的人或物。

- In Hawthorne's famous novel, the scarlet letter is a **symbol** for adultery.
  在霍桑知名的小說中，紅字是姦淫罪的**象徵**。

theme 主題

戲劇或小說的主要意義；中心思想。

- Ambition and revenge are common **themes** in Shakespeare's plays.
  在莎士比亞的劇作中，雄心壯志與報復是常見的**主題**。

tragedy 悲劇

嚴肅且有悲傷結局的戲劇。

- *Macbeth*, the shortest of Shakespeare's plays, is a **tragedy**.
  莎士比亞最短的劇作《馬克白》是部**悲劇**。

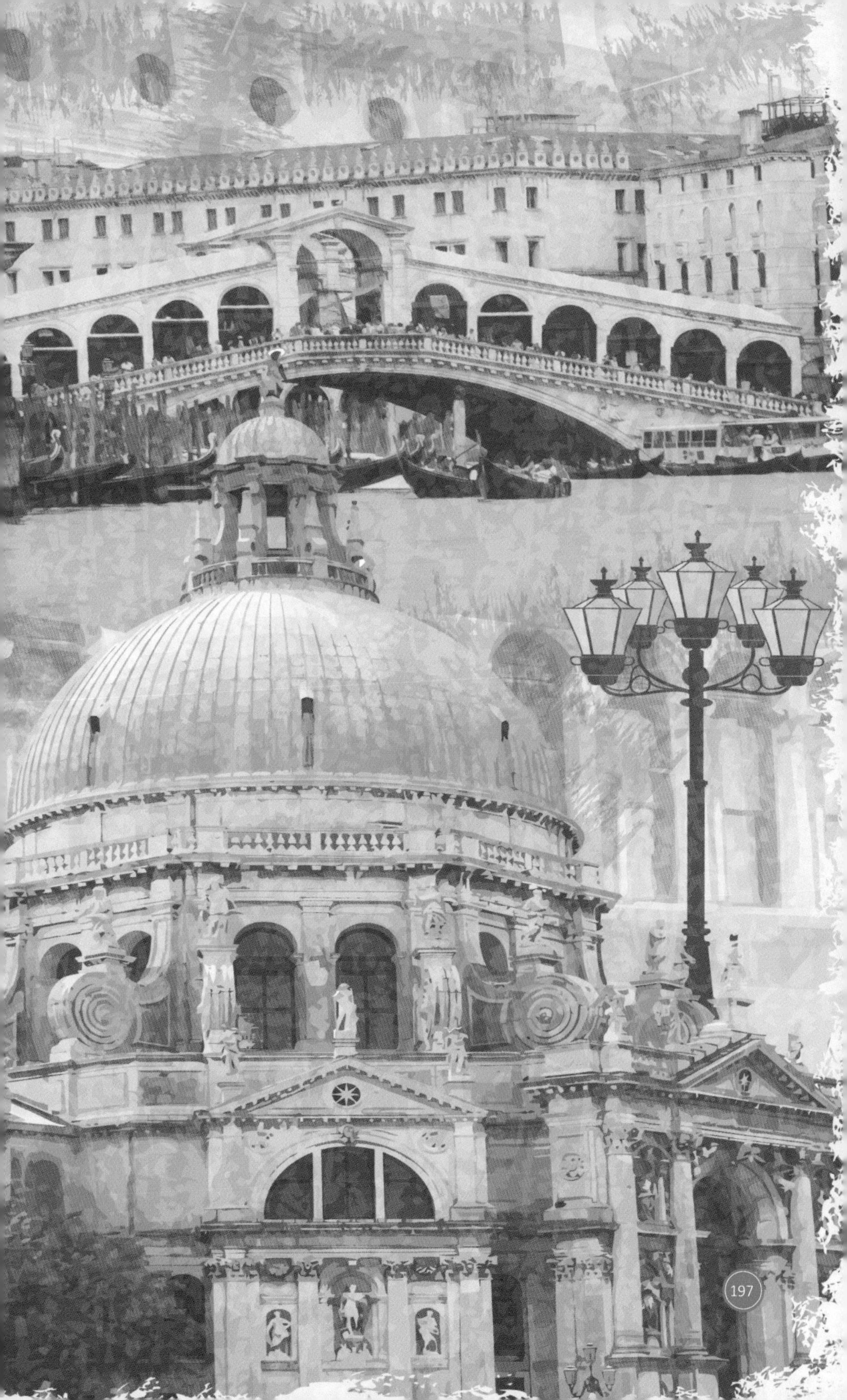